# MORONI'S CAMP
# WHERE SNAKES LURK

Look for these other exciting books by Boyd Richardson:

*Voices in the Wind,*
*Knife Thrower,*
*Danger Trail,*
and

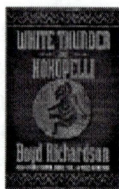

*White Thunder & Kokopelli*

# MORONI'S CAMP

# WHERE SNAKES LURK

## BOYD RICHARDSON

*Best Wishes*

*Boyd Richardson*

CAMDENCOURT
PUBLISHERS

CAMDEN COURT PUBLISHERS, INC.
PO Box 901875
Sandy, UT 84090

Moroni's Camp, Where Snakes Lurk

This is a fictional work, and as such, all characters and events portrayed in this book are fictional—with the exception of Moroni, a historical personality from the Book of Mormon—and any resemblance to real people or incidents is purely coincidental.

ISBN: 1-890828-07-6

1st Edition: Fall 1998
2nd Edition: Fall 1999

PRINTED IN THE UNITED STATES OF AMERICA.
10 9 8 7 6 5 4 3 2

This novel is dedicated to Patriarch John Erkelens, a solid church-man with the gift of healing.

Not all things in life can be explained by using logic and reason, as is brought out in this novel. Fifteen years ago I hobbled into Patriarch Erkelens's office for a blessing, hardly able to walk. I got the blessing and a week later my doctor told me that my immediate problem must have been misdiagnosed. Now I not only walk, but run marathons. May the Lord continue to bless America with men like John Erkelens.

# Contents

1. Running All Out ...................................................... 1
2. Where Snakes Lurk ................................................. 9
3. Eyes in the Night ................................................. 15
4. The Wolf Was Following Me ............................... 27
5. Down, Down, Oops! ........................................... 35
6. The Third Cried Wee, Wee, Wee .......................... 45
7. Creepy Crawler of Snake Draw ............................ 55
8. How to Die Standin' Up .................................... 71
9. The Mountain Knows No Mercy ........................... 91
10. A Quarrelsome Breeze ............................................. 99
11. Red Coals and Hot Pook ...................................... 111
12. A Tiny Sound ....................................................... 125
13. We Go Hunting ...................................................... 131
14. Suddenly My Revolver Bucked ........................... 139
15. The Lobo Loped Over the Rise ............................ 147

Special recognition goes to Ron Singer and Owen Richardson.

Ron of the Towering House Clan, Navajo Nation, gave me counsel and Owen, a gifted cousin, did the ink sketches.

# CHAPTER ONE
# RUNNING ALL OUT

The coyote dun horse had been running all out for an hour, his sides lathered and his breath coming short and ragged. Maybe I was killing the horse; it appeared so. Yet the Paiutes were pressing hard on my trail, yipping and hooting it up like a pack of hounds after a fox. I was the fox and didn't like my lot.

What riled up the Paiutes, I surely didn't know. It couldn't have been me, 'cause I'm about as threatening as a gopher, unless I get riled. Frankly I was gettin' riled, I surely was, though there was a whole pack of Indians and only one of me. Back near the Paiute village where I first met the hunting party, the odds were not good. My ma didn't raise no dummies, so when the savages showed less than a friendly countenance, I lit out like a scared rabbit.

Don't get me wrong—I ain't against Indians—just Indians on the prod. I grew up with an Indian as an older brother, a Shoshone named Walking Short. Adopted years before I was born by Papa and Mamma—Brigham and Ermalinda Harold of Manti—Walking Short was a teenager when I was a toddler. Everyone around Manti called him Billy, the name he chose as a white man's name.

My mount zigzagged its way among the junipers, dashing through the openings. If only I knew the country better, or if only I wasn't alone! I didn't start off alone; I started off with a party of eight men. When I met them, they were passing through Manti from Salt Lake, bent on exploring a better route to the Crossing of the Fathers. After they completed their mission, they turned their horses' heads home so that they could get in their crops before summer set in. But I wanted to see the area of natural bridges that the Indians told about, so I left the explorers and traveled with a young Ute as far as the natural bridges. Then he continued on and I turned back, having seen what I wanted to see.

Both Papa and Billy have repeatedly warned me that it's foolish to ride alone in new territory, but I don't ride alone very much—only when there's no one to ride with. 'Sides, if you want to see new country, you gotta go where the new country is. So there I was, on the east side of the Colorado River, smoking it over the arid mountains and riding hell-bent-for-leather, very much alone.

Dashing into the afternoon sun, I glanced up a ridge to my left and saw a string of Indians skylining themselves as they followed the ridge. They were almost parallel to me, though half a mile off. I cast a quick glance over my shoulder at the main group; I seemed to be leaving them in my dust. Even that bothered me because I had the feeling that I was being herded and I wondered what the Indians knew that I didn't know. The hair on the back of my neck seemed to stand on end. This was the worst fix I ever was in.

My coyote dun faltered. Was this the end? Was he giving out? Surely he couldn't take much more.

I felt for my Green River on my belt, reassuringly. Green River is the brand name of a knife that mountain men used during my papa's younger days. Papa and Billy never owned one themselves, as they both favored throwing knives, balanced and made to order. 'Course, Papa was raised by the Pawnee. He and Billy are both Indian in their thinking.

I'm just a white boy named Alma, a solid Mormon name. Born and raised in the Mormon settlement of Manti, I'm usually given to thought and meditation and wandering the hills, learning mountain man ways from my father and brother.

Odd that so many thoughts could pass through my head as I was clinging to my cayuse and running all-out for my life. Brother Morley, back in Manti, said that when you die your whole life flashes before your eyes.

My hand was still on my Green River. Should I sink the knife into my chest, taking my own life before the Paiute squaws had a chance at me with their sadistic tortures that would last for days? Uh-uh, I thought, answering my own question. A man can only die once and I wasn't sure I was ready to stand before Jesus having committed suicide. Brother Morley said that suicide was the same as murder in the sight of God.

Again my mount faltered and I knew the sign. He had given me all he had, even his life. "Greater love hath no man than this, that a man lay down his life for his friend," I thought, quoting the Bible. If that's true for a man, it is probably true for a horse.

The cayuse stumbled and I kicked free, hitting the ground on the run. My speed was greater than my legs could keep up with, so I crashed into a creosote bush, which broke my fall. The wild hoots of the Paiutes behind me told me that they had seen me go down.

With a quickness born of fear, I was on my feet like a big cat, running to where my mount lay in the burro grass. As I whipped my Winchester from the saddle scabbard, I glanced into my old friend's eyes. They looked big and sad, as if to say, "Goodbye, old buddy," then the horse gave a jerk and his sides stopped heaving, forever asleep.

With no time to rummage through the saddle bags for my box

of extra ammunition, I ripped the bags from the saddle on the run, 'cause seconds counted. My rifle and pistol were of the same caliber—.44—and took the same ammunition, so I never had to fumble between rifle and pistol ammunition.

The Paiutes were gonna get me, of that I was certain, but it was going to cost 'em dearly. I intended to die with my Green River in my hand, after every round of ammunition was spent.

Up ahead was a sandstone formation, a good spot to make a stand…if I could make it to the formation before the Indians made it to me. Yet I had an idea that the Indians were sure enough of themselves that they wouldn't want to shoot me in the back and risk losing the fun of torturing me.

I rounded a hump at full run and almost fell off a cliff. I was on the edge of a narrow canyon, more of a chasm than a canyon, with sheer sandstone walls dropping maybe ninety feet. The formation I had been headed for was on the other side of the chasm.

The Paiutes were closing in but taking their own good time and all I had to shield myself with were burro grass and Spanish daggers. They knew they had me, so why rush and maybe get someone killed?

Native Americans know the art of patience—believe me, they do. I have seen Billy crawl across a meadow so cautiously that even the insects didn't take notice. Every move was timed with the natural wave of the grasses, an art I could never master to Billy's satisfaction.

The afternoon sun was in my eyes, hotter'n the hubs of hell. 'Course, if it was in my eyes when I looked west, it would also be in the Indian's eyes, the only break I had. It was natural bridge country and a quarter mile to my right was a natural bridge. Maybe it crossed the chasm, maybe not…I couldn't tell. Regardless, there were boulders near the bridge where I might make a stand, so I cast a prayer in the general direction of heaven and lit out like an antelope.

There is a Paiute legend about a mountain that can only be

reached by crossing a natural bridge. It's a place of mystery and great powers inhabited only by the spirits. Once, legend says, it was inhabited by a lone paleface that came from the sunrise, the last of his race of people. It sounded like Moroni's haunt to me when first I heard of it. Moroni was the last survivor of a tribe of white Native Americans; he died around 500 A.D.

Running full speed, the heat lathered me down with sweat. The Indians hooted and I figured they might shoot me rather than allow me to make the boulders. Still, being shot is a lot better than being tortured to death.

As I closed the distance, I could see that the natural bridge crossed the chasm, but not on the level. My side of the bridge was fifteen or twenty feet down the face of the cliff. Twenty feet onto unstable rock is too far for me to jump, and the ledge I had to jump onto was small. Yet there are worse ways to die, so what the heck.

I jumped.

Landing on my feet, I didn't stay upright, but went down hard, striking my head on the stone. For a few seconds there I saw stars, then it seemed like my head was going to explode. I tried to shake it off, but was dizzy.

The dizziness bothered me the most, as the Paiutes wouldn't give me time to wait for it to wear off. Winchester in my right hand and my saddle bags with my extra box of ammunition over my shoulder, I crawled onto the bridge.

Maybe the dizziness was a godsend, 'cause I surely don't like heights, not this high of heights anyway. I was so dizzy I had to concentrate on sticking to the crown of the bridge and couldn't consider looking down. Had I looked down, I would have been terrified.

Repeatedly I uttered the smattering of a prayer as I inched my way across the bridge. If I could shake the dizziness and get across, I could make a stand.

You might think natural bridges, being made out of solid sandstone, will last forever and maybe some of them will. But natural bridges have slowly eroded over the centuries and sandstone isn't the strongest rock God made. Like the straw that broke the camel's back, there comes a time when too much weight is placed on a bridge and it falls.

As I crossed a fault line in the sandstone, I felt a slight shift and knew the bridge didn't have many more years to stand. Still I continued, because there was nothing else for me to do. But the crack started to widen and as I neared the far side, I sensed the end was close.

The knuckles of my left hand were bloody from scraping on the sandstone as I clutched onto my Winchester in a death grip while I crawled along the stone. But my headache was starting to numb and my dizziness was easing.

Echoing off the canyon walls, I heard the hoots of the Paiutes. Giving everything I had, I crawled off the far end of the bridge to a rubble strewn canyon rim. I slid behind a boulder and brought my rifle up to defend myself.

I had made it! But where had I made it to?

"*Oo'vu ninee!* (He's there)" someone yelled. They knew where I was. I understood Paiute only because I know Shoshone. Shoshone, Ute, and Paiute are almost the same language.

A warrior was crossing the bridge on the far rim, encouraged by his comrades. I'll have to hand it to him, he certainly showed bravery, though sometimes when a warrior starts showing off his bravery, his thinker becomes plumb puny. 'Course, I knew something the brave warrior didn't know: the center of the bridge was cracking.

Suddenly the warrior gave an involuntary startled cry and I saw the center of the bridge give way. As he fell, riding the center of the bridge to its final resting place, his departing exclamation echoed off the canyon walls.

Across the canyon the Indians gawked. Easily within rifle shot, I could have picked some of them off, but what would be the purpose? It would only waste ammunition.

When the reality of it all set in, I started shaking. I had presence of mind enough to duck back behind the boulder in case the

Indians changed their minds about using the rifles.

The Paiute people are a gentle lot, unless riled. My Ute friend had told me that the Paiutes in this location belonged to the Suhuh'vawdutsing (Squawbush water people) band. Don't ask me why, but the name *Paiute* is said to mean "Water Utes." Yet this isn't a pure Suhuh'vawdutsing village, they say. Rumor has it that after the Black Hawk War, disgruntled Paiutes crossed the Colorado and joined Suhuh'vawdutsing villages.

# CHAPTER TWO
# WHERE SNAKES LURK

There I crouched, about fifteen feet down from the canyon rim in a nest of boulders, safe from the Paiutes. It was an easy climb through broken boulders and the Indians seemed to lack interest in shooting at me. So up I climbed, then moaned in disappointment as I looked upon a field of prickly pears dotted intermittently with juniper trees. Both left and right ancient prickly pears grew to the rim of the canyon, anywhere they could find root. To the west a quarter mile, the cacti gave way to juniper-covered slopes, but a quarter mile through prickly pears is a long way.

Glancing back to the chasm where the natural bridge had been, my mind returned to the Indian legend of a mountain that could only be reached by a natural bridge. Surely this wasn't the mountain and the legend couldn't be true, because that would mean I was stranded. That couldn't be! I shook my head, not wanting to think of it.

I touched my tongue to my dry lips and glanced up at the heat-glazed sky. When I had grabbed my saddle bags off my coyote dun, why hadn't I snatched my canteen? My first task, I decided, was to get moisture into my body.

Shucking my Green River, I lopped off some prickly pear tunas and carefully peeled them. They weren't ripe yet, but had started to change color and I knew that if I ate very many it would give me a stomachache. Still, I plopped the pulp into my mouth. It helped with the thirst, but I still had the prickly pear patch to contend with. The shortest route appeared to be straight through, clearing a path inch by inch with my Green River and a stick. Glancing across the natural bridge, I noticed several Paiutes squatted on their haunches, watching me. They were the lingerers.

Then I dug into my saddle bags for something I could use to make a sling so that I could hang my Winchester over my back and shoulders. The best I could come up with was a scrap of pegging rope and with that I made do. Busying myself with the pegging rope, I soon created an impromptu sling. Then I threw my rifle and bags over my shoulder and turned my attention to the task of crossing the prickly patch.

Knife in hand, I laboriously cleared my way to the first juniper tree. There I broke off a limb and used that instead of my knife; it seemed to do better. The sun was three hands high in the west, shining directly into my eyes. My headache was returning, as was my dizziness, but I had no place to rest because I didn't want to lie down among the cacti.

Several times I heard the rattle of seed pods blowing in the breeze, or thought I heard them rattle. When I looked around, I couldn't see any seed pods, but in my dizziness I wasn't thinking straight.

Suddenly a skinny brown rattlesnake flashed out of the prickly pears, quicker 'an a bull whip. It struck my boots but couldn't penetrate the thick leather.

Pinning the snake to the ground, I sawed off its head, then flipped the snapping head into the prickly pears. Like a chicken that continues to run around long after his head is removed, a snake head will continue to bite long after being severed. Since the venom is in the head, you can die of a bite by a severed snake head.

There isn't much about any kind of snakes that I like, though I would have saved the tiny rattler had it contained more meat. But I had many hours of work ahead of me and no desire to hear the dead snake rattle as I worked, so I tossed the reptile into the prickly pears and heard it rattle as it landed.

Remembering the rattling I had heard earlier and assuming they were seed pods blowing in the breeze, I glanced around and saw no seed pods. Maybe the rattle wasn't pods, but rattling snakes? I shivered. Usually snakes will slip away if you make enough ruckus, but apparently the snakes in this cactus field didn't know how to behave snakelike. How many rattlers were lurking among the cacti? Dozens? Hundreds?

Turning my eyes toward heaven, I opened up in prayer the way my ma taught me. I prayed all-out, using words like "thee" and "thou," as they do in church. I don't mean to sound disrespectful of the Lord, but it seemed that God went too far when he created snakes. They have plagued mankind since the Garden of Eden.

Making as much noise as I could to warn the snakes I was coming, I continued my task. The sun had moved two hands lower in the afternoon sky. One hand roughly represents an hour, they say. 'Course, I had never owned a watch and so had not given it much studying.

Repeatedly I mopped the salty sweat from my forehead. Was I sweating from the heat or from fear of the snakes? I didn't know. Maybe I had a fever. Still it was hot enough to wither a fence post and I sure enough had more moisture to me than a fence post.

Again I heard a rattle and froze. A second tiny brown rattler was defending its turf. I could either back off, try to pin him with my stick, or blast away with my .44. Though I had a full belt of cartridges, ammunition was precious, being as I was so far away from civilization. The tiny rattler didn't seem worth it. Nor was I in the mood to pin him and sever his head, not after he so politely told me his location and gave me a chance to clear out. So I backed up a yard and struck a route around the reptile.

I cast an eye at the sun. It had advanced another three fingers. It wouldn't be long now, as most of the field was behind me.

A half hour later I stepped from the cactus field onto sandstone boulders and looked back. It hadn't been far as distance goes, but it was a task I would not like to try again.

Ahead, tobosa and yeso grew in soil so poor it looked like it wouldn't support anything 'cept horny toads. Farther west the tobosa gave way to sage brush and junipers ringed with burro grass. With a sigh of relief, I glanced at the sun setting on the western horizon. It had been a long day.

Making my way over the stones, I relaxed my snake vigil only when I reached the red soil under the junipers. Still I had to watch carefully for cacti, as the tiny pincushion cactus lurked among the sagebrush.

Striking a fire, I settled in for the night. When I bedded down, I found myself reelin' around like a pup circlin' to find a spot to lie down, creating a shoulder hole for myself and also a hip depression. As the weariness drained from my body, the last thing I remember before I slept was the odd odor of pig manure on the night breeze.

Something awakened me when the one o'clock chill set in. The Big Dipper was low in the sky, the Milky Way cut diagonally across the center of the heavens, and directly overhead Hercules stood on his head with a drawn sword. Obviously none of the constellations had awakened me. Glancing around I detected nothing, but saw that my fire was down to coals. So in one easy, fluid movement I fed it some deadfall limbs.

As the flames caught hold, I glanced to the juniper trees and glimpsed movement. Palming my .44, I slipped into the darkness, moving like a big cat.

Nothing. For thirty minutes I searched, but still nothing. A night hawk called and far to the south coyotes yammered their mournful song. I shivered, feeling alone. Really alone.

# CHAPTER THREE

# EYES IN THE NIGHT

Mouth dry and lips cracked, I struggled for reality as the birds awakened me. The moon was gone but the sky was studded with a million stars which shown so brightly that there were shadows under the trees. I wondered how the birds know when a new day is approaching, but they always seem to know. I listened to the predawn sounds and smelled the night smells. All seemed as it should except for a faint barnyard smell that I couldn't place.

I tried to go back to sleep but couldn't sleep with the racket the birds were making. Presently the sky began to fill itself with the predawn glow and as the stars faded from sight I met the new day. Slowly I made my way to the prickly pear field where I lopped off some pears and peeled them, quickly plopping the fruit into my dry mouth. Then I carried additional pears and pads back to my

fire and was singeing off the nettles when the first red arrows of
sunlight touched the trees. I continued my project and when the
pads were singed, I filled my belly. After eating the cactus I felt I
had enough moisture in my mouth to chew jerky, so I dug out a
hunk and sliced off a chew. As I chewed, I made my way to where
I had seen movement during the night. I studied the tracks.

*Wolves!*

Wolves surprised me, as I had thought this was generally
coyote country. But I was even more surprised that the wolves
were so bold. Sometimes in winter when wolves are really hungry
they'll come near a campfire, but this was early summer with food
everywhere.

Alone and without a horse, it was time for me to start the long
trek back to Manti. Putting the chasm behind to my back, I started
walking, searching for Indians and water pockets, in that order. I'd
had my fill of the cantankerous Paiutes, lost a good horse and
saddle, and nearly lost my scalp.

This was sandstone country, mostly red sandstone. White
sandstone is where you find water pockets year round, though red
sandstone has pockets that will hold water for many hours, until
the sun and wind evaporate the water.

My eyes were ever moving for signs of Paiutes as I walked. The
walking was good and I had traveled all morning, seeing no
moving creatures 'cept horny toads, jack rabbits, and birds. Up
ahead, it seemed the landscape was about to change, as in the
spaces between the junipers and sage I could see far into the west.

Suddenly my nostrils caught a whiff of smoke and I took to the
junipers like a scared rabbit. I tested the air a second time with my
nose and the odor was gone. Yet I had smelled the smoke and
knew I had.

Cautiously, I inched forward and was surprised to find myself
on the rim of a cliff. I crowded the edge, staying on the shady side
of a boulder as I peeked over the edge. It was a long drop, maybe
a hundred feet straight down, though I couldn't be sure of the
distance. How do you tell distance when looking straight down?

At the base of the cliff was a large fan of debris, as high as the cliff itself, maybe higher and farther out was a wash. The wash was lined intermittently with cottonwood trees, as are most washes in this country. Atop the fan, nestled in folds in the cliff to provide a measure of protection, was a typical bush and pole Paiute wickiup. Are the Paiutes everywhere? A man that appeared stooped with age was pulling firewood from a pile of dead driftwood in the wash.

Scanning the countryside from my vantage point, I saw no more lodges. Sometimes old men will go off by themselves to be alone and maybe die, especially when they no longer feel useful to anyone in the village. Maybe this was such a man. Clearly he didn't seem a threat, but who knows?

In the distance my eyes caught movement. Studying the spot, I saw it again—wolves, two of 'em.

Scanning the cliffs in both directions, there were no obvious routes down. To my left a quarter mile, a draw cut halfway down the cliff, but still left a formidable drop. Below the draw was a pool of water, probably the water supply for the old man.

Thinking of the water, I touched my parched tongue to my cracked lips. I needed to find water. A shadow passed over me and I glanced up to see a hawk high above me, clutching something in its claws. I studied the hawk and decided he had caught a snake.

Sliding away from the edge, I studied my options. A hundred yards to the south the cliff's rim lowered fifteen or twenty feet, forming a large horseshoe open to the western sun but protected on three sides. The sandstone would hold the heat of the sun for many hours into the night, giving me a measure of comfort, as I was without a blanket. Gathering my saddle bags and Winchester, I paused only to lop off some prickly pear pads.

I wasn't the first camper to camp in the horseshoe, which surprised me, as the area seemed so remote. There was a fire ring, big as life, dark with desert varnish. More surprising was the pictograph covering the horseshoe walls. In what seemed a progressive session of pictograph, they depicted wars between two tribes, one represented by a wide-shouldered, narrow-hipped, dark-skinned people and the other represented by light skin. In the center was pictured a man, all alone, scratching or writing on tablets and high to another side was a hunchback with a flute that appeared to be playing to the other pictographs.

"Moroni!" I said aloud, for surely the man in the center writing on tablets was Moroni and this must have been his camp.

Moroni was America's first mountain man, depending on how you define the term. Certainly he wasn't a trapper, garnering beaver pelts that satisfied the beaver hat styles of Europe. But he wandered alone, the last of his people. Apparently at least part of that time he was right here in this very camp, keeping aloof from the other inhabitants lest they kill him.

I thought of the Indian legend about a mountain that could only be reached by crossing a natural bridge. It was supposed to be a place of mystery and great powers, inhabited only by the spirits. This might be a place of mystery and great powers and it might be inhabited by the spirits, but even a mouse won't have a burrow with only one exit and surely Moroni was wiser than a mouse.

Situated on the rim of the cliffs as it was, the camp commanded an imposing view for dozens, maybe hundreds of square miles, or would have commanded such a view had not Junipers grown up on the rim of the cliff. And, I thought as I touched my parched lips, there must be water around here somewhere, else Moroni wouldn't have had such an elaborate camp.

Gathering some inner juniper bark for tinder, I hunkered down next to the fire ring and struck a small fire, then singed the needles from the cactus pads and tunas for food. In my saddle bags was antelope jerky, much too dry for me to consider chewing.

Sitting in the shade of what could be taken for a stone altar, I sucked the juice from the pears and rested. There was something strange about this camp, a peacefulness that seemed to penetrate my very soul. It made me feel like humming the songs from my childhood, hymns I hadn't thought of for months. "In our lovely

Deseret…" I hummed.

The sun set red in the west as I curled up between my fire and the stone that reminded me of an altar. In the dry sand I easily made a slight shoulder and hip hole and slept like a baby. When the one o'clock chill set in, I awoke and listened for the sounds of the night before reaching for a hunk of firewood that I had carefully placed at hand the night before. As usual, I stirred the red coals with the end of the firewood before leaving the wood nestled amongst them to catch hold, then glanced around as the light illuminated the pictographs.

Like a dip into an ice water stream, I caught my breath at what I saw, maybe a little more fearful than I would have liked to admit.

Eyes! Two eyes were sparkling at me from the edge of the firelight!

I moved, reaching for my .44 as I heard a slow snarl. I checked the load, then studied the eyes as I added sagebrush to the fire to brighten the night. A second, then a third and fourth set of eyes appeared.

Wolves, big and gray! And they didn't seem the least bit afraid of me, though they seemed respectful of the blaze. Fear gripped my chest as I backed up to the fire, adding even more wood. What would I do when I ran out of wood?

Grabbing a hunk of sagebrush, I stuck the tops in the fire and when it caught hold I charged. Far as I know, all animals will give way initially when charged with a stick, especially a flaming stick. The wolves gave way and I returned to the fire. Yet I knew they were still out there, just beyond the reaches of the firelight.

The rest of the night I slept in catnaps, not wanting to be caught by surprise by my meat-eating guests. The day dawned overcast and I was still tired. I hoped the clouds meant rain and even prayed for it. Yet I wasn't about to sit around dry mouthed, waiting for rain that may or may not come. So I climbed the highest elevation at hand and looked for signs of water—cottonwoods or a change in the color of the foliage.

To the south, several miles along the rim of the cliff, I saw what might be white sandstone formations. I gathered my gear and started in that direction.

Before reaching the white sandstone, I reached the draw I had seen the day before from the rim of the cliff, the draw that cut halfway down the cliff but still left a formidable drop. I recalled that below the drop was a pool of water, totally inaccessible to me.

The draw was littered with snake skins, the discarded shedding of rattlers, but snake skins can do you no harm. Still I was concerned because I hate snakes. I don't even care for the domestic blow snakes that residents of Manti keep around to catch the field mice.

Starting down the draw I was careful, but not overly cautious. The draw contained water at times, else the pool wouldn't exist below the cliff. Then halfway down I froze as the familiar rattle of a brown rattler met my ears.

With mixed feelings, I hated the little reptiles but was grateful to the creature for warning me. Carefully I backed up, but not before I got a good glimpse of the rocks below and saw what amounted to a community of rattlers. Though I didn't know exactly where their den was, I didn't care much. It was enough to know I was where I wasn't wanted.

Returning to the rim of the draw, I followed it away from the cliff. The draw snaked southeast into a juniper-covered hill. In the junipers the draw was shallow with gently sloping sides, not too steep for me to venture down.

Inquiring drops of rain touched my head and my hope of rain water soared. Near the bottom of the draw were red sandstone depressions that could hold water for many hours, maybe days. I cleaned them out and hastily constructed tiny dams as the probing drops turned into more serious specimens.

Sandstone country is a country of overhangs, leaving no want for a place to huddle out of the rain. Yet I was more interested in keeping my gear dry than keeping myself dry, so I stored my gear and stepped into the sprinkles. As the rain increased in intensity, I drank deeply from the murky runoff and even bathed myself.

Then I filled my tiny beat-up coffee pot with water and slid under an overhang to munch on jerked antelope as I watched the rain.

The coffee pot was a coffee pot in name only, as I didn't drink the stuff. Not that many a Mormon doesn't drink coffee, but when I tasted coffee I didn't like it. Why acquire a taste for something you don't like that is so expensive?

Into the early afternoon it rained and when it stopped, the sun came out steaming the earth with its heat. Out, too, were the desert flowers in all their glory.

A lizard zipped out from under the cactus to a sandstone slab and studied me whimsically, his little sides heaving. He tested the air, seemed to like what it contained, and zipped away.

I made my way south again, but this time I wasn't looking for water, but was on my way off the mountain to head home. Staying close to the rim, I examined every possibility of a route down and saw none. Once I found a skinny chimney that was just wide enough for a person to put his back against one side and his feet against the other. I might be able to work my way down, I thought, but I couldn't be sure that the chimney wouldn't widen out, letting me down sudden-like.

I had been walking south for a half hour when I abruptly reached a chasm that nearly took my breath away. It had sheer walls straight down for a long way, maybe a hundred feet. Though it came in from the east, I was sure it turned north and was the very chasm that I had crossed on the natural bridge. It was something to consider.

Nothing better to do, I turned east, following the chasm. When night came, I slept under an overhang, then continued in the morning. I was circling a juniper-covered mountain and by midmorning the chasm had turned north and the vegetation was running heavy with prickly pears. Circling a cactus field that was similar to the field I had hacked my way through, I didn't lose sight of the chasm. I was not surprised when I saw the remains of the natural bridge I had crossed four days earlier.

Maybe the route off the mountain was to the north. Surely

there must be a route, else Moroni couldn't have used it for his camp. Still, I wondered. Surely Moroni wouldn't have crossed the natural bridge, but maybe the natural bridge was larger in his day. But why did the Indian legend say that there was no route off the mountain?

I thought of the brave Paiute that had gone down with the bridge, remembering his scream or attempted war cry. It's a terrible thing to see a man go under, even an enemy.

A rabbit bounded across my path, but I was leery of shooting it even though I wanted fresh meat. I didn't know exactly where the Paiutes were and didn't want to advertise my position with the loud report of a pistol. If it had been a deer, I would have taken the chance of killing it. 'Course, if I saw an antelope I could run it down the way Billy taught me, though some antelope have too much stamina for a human to run down. "If you can't run them down," Billy had once said, "they are probably too tough to eat."

I continued north, skirting the prickly pear fields. I walked in burro grass but kept my eyes and ears alert for reptiles. Rodents like to live in grass, and any place there are rodents, there are likely snakes.

The sun was four hands high in the west when I found where the chasm broke in the open, met by a cliff that took off southwest. Yet I had found no route down.

I just sat there with my face in my hands, feeling sorry for myself and wondering if there was any hope. Yet I had faith that there was a route down, somewhere.

Musing, I wondered if I could make cordage from yucca, sage or juniper bark that would be strong and long enough to use as rope. The thought was scary, yet something to consider.

At least I didn't have to worry about the Paiutes, I thought as I straightened myself to full height. I would claim the next big game that crossed my tracks, though I didn't want to waste ammunition on rabbits that could be so easily trapped. I didn't know how long my supply of ammunition would last.

Shouldering my Winchester and saddle bags, I followed the

cliff rim to the southwest and was to the point where it turned south when I found a good spot to camp.

With my back to large boulders, I made two trench fires, one each direction for better defense against the wolves. This side of the mountain seemed to be where the wolves haunted. Settling in, I felt the weariness drain from my muscles. Then I slept.

When I awakened during the night to add wood to my fire, I peered long into the blackness, studying the dark spots as I added brush to my fire. Something moved, then reflected the firelight back at me.

Eyes!

It just didn't seem right that the wolves would be watching me, though there was only one set. No siree, it didn't make sense. No sense at all. Adding more fuel to the fire, I slept again, but kept dreaming of the eyes. The wolves were out there. Watching. Waiting.

Twice in the next ten days I made rounds of my mountain prison, carefully searching for a way down the cliffs. I found nothing.

Setting snares netted me several rabbits. But the wolves robbed more of the rabbits from my snares than I got. As soon as the rabbit squealed, as rabbits often do when dying, the wolves had them. The wolves were becoming a nuisance, threatening my food supply.

I made Moroni's camp my camp, fortifying it as best I could from my fleet-footed, carnivorous friends. Yet I noticed that when the wolves came around, they didn't bother me. They only watched curiously.

Sometimes when I got lonely I would belly up to the edge of the cliff and see what the old man was doing below. On the morning of my nineteenth day on the mountain I was watching him set snares for rabbits. Suddenly he startled a sleeping doe that jumped to her feet with a lurch and bounded through the trees, crossing the wash and running parallel to the cliff directly below me.

Initially, the old Indian whipped an arrow out of his quiver and attempted an offhanded shot at the deer. The shot missed, badly.

I don't know why I did it—just for the heck of it I guess—but as the deer passed beneath me I drew a bead on her, wondering if I could judge the bullet drop accurately from my angle. I was shooting almost straight down as I squeezed off a round and felt the rifle buck in my hands. I must have severed her spine 'cause she dropped in her tracks.

Casting my eyes in search of the old Indian, I couldn't find him. Yet I knew he was somewhere close, concealed in the trees. I was sure that in the fifteen days that I had been camping near him, he must have smelled my fire once or twice, so he probably had a good idea that someone was around. I knew he would find the deer, so I slid from the rim and went my way.

Back at camp, I settled in for the evening. Loneliness was heavy upon me and I found myself remembering my boyhood back in Manti. I remembered Mama and Papa and Billy and the old gang that I grew up with. There was a girl back home named Temperance Deloach, who was just a pesky little thing when we were children, but we had both grown up and in doing so she filled out her clothes in all the right places. Like a lone coyote howling at the moon, I leaned back and sang "They're Tenting Tonight On the Old Camp Grounds."

# CHAPTER 4
# THE WOLF WAS FOLLOWING ME

It hadn't rained for ten days and a good shower was long overdue to my way of thinking. My water supply was down to nearly nothing.

I had spent the last ten days searching for a route off the mountain and decided it was time for me to spend a few days looking for Moroni's water supply, hoping that it still existed. Even if it had dried up, I wanted to know where it had been.

The day's search would begin at the top of the juniper-covered mountain east of Moroni's camp, I decided. If nothing else, I could get a higher view of my prison.

As I sat in Moroni's camp making plans, I suddenly realized that a female wolf was approaching. I was surprised that her approaching didn't bother me. Maybe that was because I was ready to die, if that was in store for me. It seemed I was helplessly trapped, so why not?

On further consideration I recalled that wolves didn't always kill their prey before they started eating them. No, I thought. I changed my mind. Slowly I palmed my .44 and waited.

The female wolf, the size of a large dog, stepped to the edge of my camp, then just stood there, watching. She didn't look undernourished nor did she look like she was on the prowl for dinner.

"*Maik'w peah'suhnuv* (hello, big coyote)," I greeted. In all of the Native American languages that I am familiar with, wolves are called either big coyotes or coyotes are called little wolves. In the Paiute culture, the creator is a wolf, but he is called *Toovuts*. Braves who have the power of the wolf are thought to be cunning and strong and when a wolf comes to your camp, it's a good sign. The wolf just watched me and I watched her as the sun moved two fingers in the sky. Then she turned and walked off.

Moroni's camp sometimes seemed like such a peaceful spot that it felt almost sacred. What had the Indian legend said? Oh yes, it was a place of mystery and great powers, inhabited by the spirits. It certainly was a place of mystery, but the spirits that haunted it, if indeed the place was haunted, seemed to be friendly, spirits like would go to church come Sunday. When I relaxed around the camp, I often wanted to stay put and meditate, as if I were in a tabernacle or temple.

"What am I doing?" I asked myself, realizing I had wiled away a full hour. "At least I could gather my big feet under me and go find where Moroni got his water. There's no use sitting here, drying up with thirst!"

Rising to my feet, I threw my trappings on my shoulder and moved out. I didn't have a trail to follow; I just wandered up the mountain, threading my way between the junipers, sage, and cacti. But why didn't I have a trail? Surely Moroni would have beaten a path to water, wherever it was. I studied the earth, imagining I was seeing signs of trails everywhere. At last I shook my head to clear it.

As I walked, I was suddenly aware of the female wolf following me. When I stopped, she stopped. And when I started walking again, she started. I checked the load in my .44 then checked the load in my rifle.

For almost three hours I hiked, always going up. A juniper had planted itself on the very top of the mountain, making it so that I didn't have to skyline myself when studying the terrain.

Far to the east, maybe five miles or so, were several ribbons of smoke. Probably the Paiute village, I thought. I brought my gaze closer and detected a brightness in the color of the greenery a half mile east of me.

"Wolf," I called, addressing the female wolf that was forty feet down my backtrail, "is that where Moroni got his water?"

The wolf cocked her head to one side. But, of course, wolves can't speak.

Excitement began to grow within me, 'cause it seemed that at last I was going to find water and less than a mile away. Making my way through the junipers, bearing to the left as I descended, I was brought short as I entered a clearing and view spot.

A building!

Well, more of a dugout than a real building—it was a sorry looking structure. Stones had been placed on top of each other using yeaso as mortar. Yeaso is a pure white substance much like clay. When cooked and mixed with sand and water, it becomes mortar. Sandstone slabs had been placed on the top and dirt heaped above that. Eyeing the sandstone slabs, I muttered to the female wolf, "It took a lot of men to lift those slabs in place." The wolf cocked her head to one side, as if she liked having someone talk to her.

The dugout had a rawhide door, but with further investigation I learned the rawhide was covering something, probably wood. It appeared to have been closed from the inside and looked like a good place for snakes to crawl, though I had to admit that there were fewer signs of snakes as I neared the top of the mountain.

I started to push on the door, but thought better of it. I'd return to explore the structure when I had made several good torches. My current project was to find water, not explore a guard shack.

Looking down at the greenery less than a mile away, I had a commanding view. Not much farther beyond the greenery was the spot where the natural bridge had been, and far in the distance, across the great chasm, was another tiny spot of greenery, maybe the corn and melon fields of the Paiute village. I needed to be on my way.

Making my way to the greenery, I followed a water course, 'cause it was easier walking. The route was fairly steep with a thirty-foot drop near the base of the mountain. As I reached the drop-off, I found myself looking down into sparking water.

A water pocket!

The sides of the water pocket were white...white sandstone. There was evidence that at one time the far end had been bricked up, allowing the pocket to store more water than it currently stored.

Taking a roundabout route to reach the bottom of the drop, I came upon the water pocket from the lower side. Fishing into my saddle bags, I pulled up my tiny beat-up coffee pot, dipped it into the cool water, and drank deeply.

Seating myself on the edge of the water tank, I felt content. Overhead Father Sun, a term both Billy and Papa used occasionally, seemed to be smiling down on me, occasionally playing peek-a-boo behind tiny pillow clouds. A slight breeze touched my face with gentle fingers. I closed my eyes and smelled the sweet air; it seemed to carry the odor of corn tassels.

The female wolf brought me back to reality as she zipped up to the water hole, careful to stay as far away from me as she could get, and started lapping at the refreshing liquid.

"So this is where you got your water, old girl," I muttered.

She cast me a sidewise glance, apparently sensing that I was talking to her, and continued lapping.

I moved to a nearby boulder and seated myself, studying the

greenery. It was a field of some type and in the center was a stone structure about six feet tall. From my vantage point, I could see two sides of the structure and both had steps. I wouldn't be surprised if all four sides had steps.

"A *rameumptom!*" I said to the female wolf, which was the same as saying it to myself.

*Rameumptom* is an ancient American name for a place to pray or preach, sort of a tower. It doesn't make sense, I know, because who wants to pray on a tower?

A tiny village must have been here once. Obviously that had been before Moroni's time, because during Moroni's time, at least when the last of the pictographs at Moroni's camp were made, he was pictured alone.

Maybe the mountain had been sort of a command post or way station before the civilization was destroyed. And when Moroni was alone wandering the mountains as a lonely mountain man, he made his way back here, looking for a secure hideout.

Studying the field, the wild crops looked familiar. Moving off the boulder where I had been sitting, I walked closer.

Corn.

The stalks were large enough, but the ears were tiny, only two inches. They weren't yet ripe, but would be in a few weeks. Weeks earlier, on the far north end of the mountain near the cliffs, I had seen some Indian rice, but even tiny ears of corn were far better than wild rice. Things were looking up.

Two days later I once again ascended the mountain, this time with several well-made torches in hand, intent on exploring the lookout dugout. Again the female wolf followed me. Though she was continually following me, I enjoyed her companionship.

I puffed my way up the mountain, weaving through the juniper trees to the lookout point where the sentry's dugout was located. Far to the east were tiny ribbons of smoke, maybe from the cooking fires from the Paiute village, though generally Indians use tiny, nearly smokeless fires for cooking. I realized I was harboring hateful feeling for the Suhuh'vawdutsing band of "Pie-

Utes," as the whites called them. The Paiutes called themselves "Pa-Utches." I didn't like to find fateful feelings within me, not for a whole tribe; I had been taught better than that.

Leaving my gear in a stack, I pushed gently on the door, then harder. It gave a little, but clearly it was going to take more force. Putting my shoulder to it, I gave it everything I had and it gave with a snap, almost toppling me into the structure.

Standing back, I struck a spark into juniper bark and lit a torch. Then, ever so carefully, I pushed the door further open.

Sticking the torch through the opening I had made, I peered through the opening, scanning the floor for any signs of reptiles. I saw nothing but dust and odds and ends of pottery, so I pushed the door inward and scanned the room again. Only then did I push the door all the way open. Poking my head in, I looked, scanning the floor, walls, ceiling, everything visible, before committing myself to stepping inside.

In the center was a type of stone table and around the room were the odds and ends of what a sentry might collect. But what surprised me most was a bow and a quiver of arrows on the table. It was a cottonwood bow and the arrows were hollow reed arrows with fire-hardened wooden tips.

Paiute arrows! There was a possibility that the arrow tips were poisoned, so I didn't touch them.

So the Paiutes had been here too, I mused. Fact is, I thought as I caught my breath over seeing something in the back of the room, they're still here!

Resting on a mat in the back of the dugout was a skeleton—not a sickly man more dead than living, but a longtime dead man whose body was reduced to a skeleton, covered with a layer of mummified hide. His dress was clearly Paiute.

I was disappointed, really disappointed. Maybe I expected to find some old breast plates, or even some brass cooking vessels, but all I found was a relatively modern skeleton of a Paiute. Maybe he had been dead fifty or sixty years—surely not much longer, if any. Of course, I had found a house relatively free of snakes where

I could spend the winter once I swept out the cobwebs and buried the Paiute, but I intended to find a route off the mountain long before winter, for sure.

One last look around, making sure that I hadn't missed anything that might be useful to my survival, and I stepped out, pulling the door closed as best I could to protect the remains of the skeleton from the wolves.

Wolves? Now that was an interesting thought. Where were they, anyway? I cast a questioning glance at the female wolf. "Where is your pack?" I asked. She cocked her head to one side, dog-like.

## CHAPTER 5
# DOWN, DOWN, OOPS!

More of a slit in the rocks than a chimney, the shaft I had labeled a chimney appeared to be my only possible escape option. Repeatedly I looked it over, studying it from every angle I could. It appeared to be about the same width, two to three feet wide, all the way down. Just as easy as falling off a log, I thought, yet the word "falling" seemed to stick in my craw. I shook my head to clear it, for surely I had to have faith in my own abilities or I'd spend the rest of my life as a prisoner on this snake-infested mountain.

If I didn't have my gear to contend with, I'd be able to make the descent. I'd just brace my back against one side and my feet or knees against the other, then work my way down. If the chimney proved impassible, I'd simply walk back up the same way.

To lower my gear down the chimney, I'd need a long rope. As

a youth I'd seen ropes made many a time out of hemp and I could whip out a length of cordage quicker 'an scat once I got my fingers nimbled up. 'Course, I'd only made five or ten feet lengths, not a hundred-foot length.

The idea seemed so pleasing to me that I set right to work with yucca fibers, making a long cordage. It took me the rest of the day and more. Then I took my cordage to the chimney and measured it for length using a weighted stone.

Next I made another and still another cordage and I kept making them. When I ran out of yucca, I made some out of the inner bark of the juniper. Then lastly, weeks later, I made all my cordages into one long rope.

While working on the rope, I enjoyed the periodic company of the female wolf. She seemed to follow me all the time, everywhere I went. But as time passed I began wondering what happened to the other wolves. I had seen six of them at one point. And the number of rabbits being robbed from my snares had dropped off to almost nothing. Something seemed terribly wrong.

One day I was so curious that I put aside my rope and made my way to the wolf den. I had not been to the den because the wolves and I aren't on a first name basis, but I had a general idea where it was. The female wolf followed me as she always did. Yet I was careful, 'cause you don't always like a wolf at your heels.

I smelled the stench of death before I saw them, outside in their den. Circling, I approached from the upwind side. What I saw was not pretty, not pretty at all.

Five dead wolves, bloated with blow flies. I stripped some inner juniper bark and slapped it to my nose to breathe through in an effort to cut the stench and approached carefully. At first I could see no reason why the wolves died, then something caught my attention.

Fang marks!

Somewhere nearby was probably an equal number of dead rattlesnakes. Seems the wolves had stumbled on a rattlesnake den and had come out the losers.

Searching for answers I asked myself what kept the snake population on this mountain in balance. Whatever it was, it was losing ground, as the snakes seemed to be reproducing faster than any other critter. 'Course, I was a newcomer, a Johnny-come-lately, so I didn't know. I just read the signs as best I could.

Snakes don't like to be pushed around. 'Course, none of us likes to be pushed around, but we aren't like snakes. Some Indian tribes feather the snakes and treat them gently—stroke 'em with feathers and make 'em more or less passionate. They say that a feathered serpent makes a good pet, but I ain't about to have a snake for a pet, even a blow snake. No siree, give me something safe, like a grizzly with a sore tooth.

Maybe the female wolf was visiting me when her pack battled it out with the reptiles, maybe not. Still, she was alone just like me...alone on a mountain crawling with rattlesnakes.

Trudging back to Moroni's camp, it seemed the wolf stayed closer than before. We were a pack of two.

By the time I had finished the rope, the wild corn was ripening. For days I munched on fresh corn and roasted rabbit, getting up the nerve for my descent down the chimney.

Several times I trudged to the *rameumptom* and prayed atop it. Yet it didn't seem to hold the sacred reverence in my heart as did Moroni's camp. The pictograph of the lone figure writing on some type of tablets touched my inner feelings the most. I was alone, though not with the intensity that Moroni was alone. Had snakes taken over this mountain when Moroni was here? I thought not.

Then one day I made another startling discovery while examining some strange tracks. I discovered that they were pig tracks. That meant that there were wild pigs that lived in the wetter lands around the *rameumptom*, though I hadn't seen them. Judging by their prints, they were the size of domestic weaner pigs. On further discovery I discovered that there was even a pig wallow several dozen yards north of the *rameumptom*.

Pigs seemed the ideal creatures to live on a mountain of rattlesnakes, as pigs are generally considered immune to snake bites by virtue of their body fat. Fact is, pigs eat snakes. Many a family blow snake, used as a mouser around Manti, has met its death by encroaching on the family pig's domain. Returned missionaries to Manti say that in the Southern states they raise pigs primarily to keep down the poisonous snake population.

I named the female wolf She-Wolf 'cause that was what she was. As usual, She-Wolf followed me to the chimney the day I picked to make my descent. In a way it was a little sad having to leave her, not only because we had become friends, but because she was being left alone on the mountain. Wolves are social creatures.

Tying all my gear to the end of my rope, I lowered it to the bottom of the chimney. Then I tied the end of the rope to a juniper in case I didn't make it down and had to retrieve the gear.

"Goodbye, friend," I said to She-Wolf. She cocked her head to one side as I spoke and as I started down into the hole, she whined, sensing I was going for good. It almost broke my heart, but I certainly couldn't take the wolf with me.

This was easier than I had figured. Yes siree, in a few minutes I would be free.

I had lowered myself about eight feet when I felt a few pebbles fell on me from above. Looking up I saw She-Wolf straining to see me. She was whining. A lump seemed to be growing in my throat, but it passed.

I had descended twenty feet when I noticed the chimney was widening. There was light coming in from the side, as it wasn't a true chimney but a crack that I was climbing down. In the dim light I could see that the crack opened up wider than I could stretch, for about ten or fifteen feet. Then it returned to its normal width.

I'd have to go back!

Though it wasn't hot, the palms of my hands were sweating. Placing them firmly against the wall, I began to push myself back up the chimney, but going up was harder than I had figured. The surface of the stone began to slough off and I realized it was actually getting slick against my back. I was sliding.

Pushing even harder I gave it all I had. This seemed to help because I stopped sliding, and after a moment my muscles began to quiver and knew I was weakening. Again I strained, for my very life depended on it. I wanted to relax my muscles for just a minute, but to relax meant to fall. I glanced up and knew that just keeping from falling wasn't enough. I had to start climbing again.

A wave of panic spread over me, but if I panicked I would surely die. Gritting my teeth, I willed the panic to leave, replacing it with a prayer. "Dear God," I prayed. "I've made an awful mistake! Save me!"

Maybe the prayer helped, I'm not sure. I was forcing my muscles to give all they had, even more than they had. Sweat was running down my face and I was straining with all I had, pouring on sheer willpower, I felt myself progressing upward, inch by inch.

Suddenly my hand slid and I almost fell. From up above I heard a whine. It was She-Wolf pleading with me, encouraging me.

I had to wipe the slick blood from my hands, else I would fall. Bracing myself with my back against one wall and my feet against the other, I freed my hands and wiped my palms on my shirt, leaving the shirt smeared with blood.

"Jesus! Help me!" I cried. It was the cry of a man about to die.

Feet against one wall and back against the other, I could only rest my hands and arms, not my legs and back.

"Help me!" I cried again, for I knew I was losing my battle with the chimney. Then from somewhere up above came a voice, not a loud voice but it had the ring of authority in it.

"Hold onto the rope, Alma, and pull yourself up," the voice said.

Glancing up I saw a man standing there. He wasn't a large man, at least not as large as Papa and he had a rather large head. For just an instant the name Moroni flashed through my brain and I figured it was him, or at least his ghost.

"The rope isn't strong enough to hold me," I replied.

"Have faith, Alma. The Lord hasn't forsaken you."

Making the supreme effort, I tried not to doubt. Instead I took hold of the rope and pulled, though I didn't put all my weight on the rope by pushing with my feet as I pulled.

I didn't know when I reached the rim until I felt the sun on my face. Then I pulled myself to safety and just lay there, shaking. The next thing I knew the sun was in my eyes and She-Wolf was licking my face, much like a domestic dog.

"Moroni," I muttered as I looked around. But there was just She-Wolf.

"Moroni," I muttered again as I sat up and gave the area better scrutiny. Still, he was gone.

Gathering my feet under me, I counted myself happy to be alive. I wasn't alone, at least not all alone. I had She-Wolf and Jesus, though I didn't have my freedom. But is any man really free? All men are tied to their land, their jobs, or their sins.

I trudged home to Moroni's camp. Over my shoulder I carried my saddle bags and rifle and my long length of rope. I watched as a hawk swooped to the earth and rose again with a dangling rattler. The hawks knew how to put rattlesnakes to good use. Maybe I should start eating rattlers, I thought. It wouldn't be so bad if the rattlers were the big, meaty variety that you see around Manti.

Sweat was trickling down my back. It was high time for me to take a bath and wash my clothes. A good supper of fresh corn would taste good, too, I thought.

Leaving my gear at camp, I took my coffee pot and a basket I had made for toting the two inch cobs of corn and shuffled over the hill for water and corn. I had worn a path through the burro grass, around the pin cushion cacti and sagebrush, between the junipers, around the boulders and up to my water supply.

After tanking up on the refreshing liquid, I bathed and cleaned my linen shirt. My pants were buckskin and you don't normally wash buckskin, though you can if you want. You clean them by rubbing them down with clay, preferably white clay.

While my shirt was drying, I picked my way to the *rameumptom* and spent a while at prayer. Then I set to work picking a basket of corn for supper. I had already picked the corn that was easy to reach at the edge of the field, so I had to venture farther inward.

Suddenly I heard a squeal from almost under my feet that raised the hair on the back of my neck and cheated me out of a year's growth. A fat little squealing pig took off through the corn with a speed that reminded me more of a jackrabbit.

But I was in big trouble 'cause a tiny wild boar, no bigger than a large rabbit, came charging at me out of who-knows-where with a gosh awful squeal that sounded like the imps in hell. I palmed my .44 and let the charging boar close in.

I had recovered from the initial shock and was imagining the taste of roast pig. I was ready and would have had the pig too, had not She-Wolf, thinking I was in danger, charged the wild boar. The two tangled not fifteen feet from me, both fighting with amazing but deadly speed.

Though She-Wolf was trying to save my life, I was afraid she would get hurt and I didn't want to lose her. So I sacrificed a bullet by firing into the air, hoping the report would break up the fight. It worked.

As if by mutual consent, the little boar fled deeper into the corn field and She-Wolf ran for safety in the juniper-covered hills.

"She-Wolf," I called, repeatedly. But she was terrified, having never heard the discharge of a revolver before.

For a long while I waited for her to return, but she didn't. Finally I trudged back to Moroni's camp alone, knowing my friend knew her way home. On the way I lopped off some prickly pear pads to use as a poultice for She-Wolf's wounds when she returned.

I built a fire, singed off the needles from the pads, ate my supper and waited for She-Wolf. When the sun set, she still hadn't returned, so I went to sleep, alone.

The one o'clock chill had not yet set in and the sandstone still held a little heat from the previous day's sun when I felt something cold on my face. She-Wolf had returned, giving credence to the term "kiss and make up."

Throwing a piece of sage on the fire for instant light, I stroked my wolf gently. Then in the light of the fire I cut the prickly pear pods in half and treated her wounds.

# CHAPTER 6
# THE THIRD CRIED WEE WEE WEE

"Three little piggies went to market," I muttered to She-Wolf. "The first little piggy had roast beef. The second had none. The third cried wee, wee, wee all the way home."

We were trudging over the mountain to the water tank and in my mind were thoughts of barbecued pig. Fact is, I had already dug a steam pit back at camp, lined it with stones and had a fire going, heating the rocks to barbecue temperature. Yep, barbecued pig was what I wanted and pig was what I'd have. Yet they weren't harmless weaner pigs, but wild boars, similar to what I'd heard tell lived in Louisiana and eastern Texas. I'd have to be careful, but I hadn't gotten myself in my present fix by being ridiculously careful—just plain careful was good enough.

I wasn't trying to teach nursery rhymes to She-Wolf, of course, but was making noise to warn the snakes that I was coming so they could get out of my way. I was learning to live in harmony with the reptiles; they warned me by rattling and I warned them by making noise. Yet it was a tense relationship for me, not one to my liking.

Over the mountain I trudged, enjoying the breeze on my face and occasionally swatting a pesky insect. Clusters of white pillow clouds occasionally cast refreshing shadows across the mountain, which was all right with me.

When we reached the edge of the corn, I told She-Wolf to stay put. "Just stay out of it!" I ordered, looking her squarely in the eye. 'Course, she didn't pay me more than passing acknowledgment 'cause she's just an animal without superior knowledge, like us humans.

Rifle in hand I trudged to the *rameumptom* for an elevated view of the most likely spot to hunt the wild hogs. I was overlooking the pig wallow several dozen yards due north, so where I sat wasn't a bad spot for me to wait. If only I could get the pillow clouds to stay put directly above me.

I heard them before I saw them, two little boar pigs that sounded less than happy with each other. They were squealing and snorting next to the pig wallow, but all I could see was the movement of the grass and corn stocks. They were making so much noise that even She-Wolf was concerned and bound up the steps of the *rameumptom* so that she could find some measure of safety by my side.

I didn't want the wolf so close 'cause I knew she would be scared when I fired the rifle and maybe run off again. But it was her decision, so I sat with my Winchester poised, ready to claim my—our—dinner.

Then the two boars finally broke out into the open and I gained an appreciation for their ferocity. She-Wolf didn't like it at all, as her wounds had still not fully healed from her last encounter. I had tried to use prickly pear poultices on her wounds, but she had been uncooperative about that. Were she in with a wolf pack, another wolf would have licked her facial wounds for her. As it was, her wounds looked awful, but they were healing.

Finally one of the little boars broke and ran, and my Winchester spoke. Both boars disappeared into the corn stocks, but I knew I had shot one 'cause I usually hit what I aim at.

She-Wolf let out a yelp as if she had been hit and out of the corner of my eye I saw her clear the *rameumptom* in a bound. Turning my full attention her direction, I saw she was running flat out. Yet from experience I knew she would come around once she had time to think it over.

Holding my .44 in readiness, I made my way to the edge of the pig wallow and followed the blood through the grass and stocks. The pig had dropped after twenty feet, but I was almighty careful before I bent over the little fighter. Green River in hand, I slit the animal's throat then triumphantly started back to camp with my trophy.

She-Wolf was back at camp when I got there, so I shared with her the parts of meat that she liked best. Then I placed my share out of her reach as I prepared to barbecue what remained of the pig.

Cleaning the coals from the steam pit, I lined it with prickly pear pads with needles scorched off. On that I placed the pig, stuffed with wild onions, herbs, and Indian rice. Then I topped it off with more layers of prickly pear pads. Covering it all with ashes, hot rocks and dirt, I let it cook all night.

The next morning I was up before the sun, observing the Great Silence more or less Indian style. The Great Silence is that period of time before the sun rises but after it is light. It is a time of personal prayer for the braves in many of the plains tribes, a sweet hour of prayer when everything in nature, even the animal tribes and Earth Mother herself, seems to stand still and pray in their own way. The only exception is Earth Mother's music makers, the bird tribe, which provides sacred music for the prayers.

'Course, I couldn't enjoy my meal with She-Wolf's big eyes glued to my every bite, so before I uncovered the barbecue the next morning, I checked my snares and returned home with a tiny rabbit for my friend. Then I set to work uncovering my feast layer by layer.

After I had removed all the dirt, rocks, and ashes, I carefully removed the layers of prickly pear pads. Then I hunkered down beside the steam pit, picking hunks of juicy meat right off the bones and stuffed them into my mouth. That was real eating, giving meaning to the term "high on the hog." 'Course, I ate the whole hog high and low, 'cept what She-Wolf ate.

It wasn't that I was unhappy on the mountain nor ungrateful to Heavenly Father for my life and the companionship of She-Wolf. But that wasn't exactly the way I wanted to spend the remainder of my days. I had repeatedly examined all the escape routes, circled the rim of the cliffs many times, and knew my options. It was early August and my family back in Manti would be worrying about me. The corn harvest was fast drawing to a close and I'd either have to store some corn for winter or get down the cliffs.

My inner drive for interaction with other humans had become so strong that in the early days of the corn harvest I had made a basket and lowered some fresh corn to the Paiute below the cliff. I really caught him off guard, I surely did.

When I lowered the basket, I was able to place it close, maybe only ten feet from the Indian's wickiup. He came out of his lodge with a bound and his eyes followed the rope up to where I was peering down. Then, lowering his gaze to the basket, he reached for the hunk of bark I had placed atop the corn. The bark contained two pictographs: one of a man giving a gift to another and the other of a man dumping the corn in a pile.

Well, that Indian studied the pictograph for a while then dumped the corn in a pile and I drew up the empty basket. Two days later I again lowered another basket of corn and on that occasion the Paiute sent up a gift of a stone knife. 'Course, I had no use for a stone knife, but it was nice to know he appreciated the corn.

Repeatedly searching the rim of the cliffs, I became convinced that my only escape route lie in Snake Draw, the draw I was afraid to encroach. From a spot on the cliff rim, a quarter mile south of the draw, I had a good look at a dry waterfall. There, runoff from Snake Draw spilled over the cliffs during a downpour and fell more or less fifty feet. At the bottom was the Paiute's source of water, a pool in the wash. The pool always contained water, or so it appeared. I had never seen it dry.

In my mind a plan was festering, a plan that included the unthinkable. I would descend into Snake Draw!

Yet I wasn't about to go down Snake Draw twice. I had faith I could make the escape the first time and I'd rely on that faith. And I wasn't going to take She-Wolf with me either 'cause she'd just get into trouble.

Yes siree, I had thought it all out. I'd lower She-Wolf to the base of the cliff and set her free. My only problems were that I didn't know how to make her hold still while I lowered her nor how to get her to untie the rope once she was down.

Then I thought of the Paiute. Would he think it was a trick? Would he set free a wild creature, a wolf that might turn on him? I wondered, yet had to take the chance.

I needed a gift for the Paiute, something that would be well received by him. Something rare and special.

A wild hog!

Returning to the *rameumptom*, I laid wait for a hog, this time for two days. The afternoon of the second day I was about to head back to camp when I heard a rustle in the corn stocks not far from me. A hog was rooting about, very actively doing something. I could just catch glimpses, but I saw enough to lay my sights on it and squeeze off a round.

Carefully I made my way to the kill and what I saw was quite surprising. The hog, a large female, had just killed a rattlesnake, which was why it was making so much noise. Otherwise she would have slipped by me unnoticed. Maybe hogs had been slipping past me unnoticed all day.

She-Wolf thought the hog belonged to the both of us when I took it home, but she was wrong. I lowered the prize in a basket to the Paiute below.

As the basket descended, the Paiute came out of his lodge. Lifting the bark with the pictograph, he jumped back, apparently surprised. Carefully he examined the kill from all angles and read the pictographs, which contained only a picture of one person giving a gift to another. After a while he carefully lifted the hog from the basket and took it inside his lodge, probably to get a gift to exchange for the hog. But in that instant I drew up the basket.

The next time I lowered the basket it contained the knife he had given me, along with a pictograph of a man cutting the ropes that bound a dog. I didn't know how to draw a pictograph of wolf, but to me they look the same as a dog.

While the Indian was holding the stone knife and pictograph, I drew up the basket, much to his surprise. Then it was She-Wolf's turn. Maybe it would work, maybe it wouldn't.

I had made a harness for She-Wolf and she submitted to the harness, though with a few questioning glances. Then I tied her feet and she didn't like that, but didn't make too much fuss. Last, I tied my pegging string around her face as muzzle. She really didn't like that, but I had the upper hand and tied her good and solid.

To keep from falling, I tied myself to a juniper tree that seemed to grow out of the cliff, and noticed that I was wet with sweat. She-Wolf looked at me through wondering, accusing eyes, a sad look that broke my heart.

Settling myself into a good lifting position, I lifted She-Wolf, swung her out and over the cliff, and started to lower her. She didn't like it, not one bit. But I had her bound good and she still had a measure of trust for me.

Hand over hand I lowered her as the Paiute watched from below. Once she swung against the side of the cliff and I felt movement on the rope as she struggled a little, then settled down.

I wondered what the Paiute was thinking. Obviously he could

see it was something like a dog or a wolf, and by the time the bundle got close, he was no doubt positive it was a wolf. Yet all Indian tribes are use to training all sorts of wild animals and from my view point, a hundred feet straight up, he seemed to take it all in stride.

First he cut the rope, allowing me to draw it up. Then he cut the harness. Last of all he cut the cords that bound the wolf's feet and a few of the cords that I had tied around the wolf's muzzle. Then he stepped back, positioning himself so that his fire was between himself and the wolf and waited. From somewhere he had retrieved a prayer stick and was holding it in front of him toward She-Wolf as the soft strains of a soothing chant drifted up to me.

Pawing, She-Wolf worked the pegging string from her muzzle, dragging her muzzle on the ground, trying to rub off the remaining ropes. When at last she was free, she stood facing the Paiute. From my position it looked like she was snarling.

The Paiute continued with the chant, but with his free hand drew a hunk of burning sagebrush to him. Slowly the wolf backed up, unwilling to turn her tail on the Paiute, fascinated by him. I wondered why she didn't just turn tail and dash for freedom.

It seemed that the Paiute was talking to She-Wolf, as one man talks to another. She stopped snarling and it seemed that she was inching herself back a little. Then she suddenly whirled and dashed down the fan that led to the wash. But before slipping between the cottonwood and juniper trees, she seemed to stop and look up at me. It was as if she were saying goodbye.

"Goodbye, old friend," I muttered, then dabbed at my eyes. When I looked up again, she had disappeared.

The sun was still two hands high in the west as I turned from the cliff, making my way back to Moroni's camp. I was thrilled She-Wolf was free, yet I was alone, really alone. As I approached Moroni's camp from a distance, I saw a rattlesnake making his way across the sand where I usually slept.

I was so amazed I stopped in mid-stride. Was no place sacred?

Were the snakes literally taking over every square inch of the mountain? As I watched, the rattler made his way closer to the pictograph of Moroni writing on the tablets.

So intent on the snake as I was, I didn't see the hawk until it struck. One second the snake was there and the next it was in the talons of a hawk, being lifted into the sky.

Many Indians believe that hawks are good signs. Never before had I formed an opinion of that, one way or another, but suddenly I had.

Hawks are good signs!

## CHAPTER 7
# CREEPY CRAWLER OF SNAKE DRAW

The awful feeling of loneliness spread over me and I didn't sleep well. Repeatedly I awoke, put wood on the fire, and looked for snakes. As the firelight flickered on the pictographs, they seemed to dance. The characters were looking directly at me—studying me. Did they approve?

Mentally I went over my plans. Hopefully I would lower myself over the cliff where the cliff was the shortest: from the bottom of Snake Draw. I had created a length of cordage to lower my Winchester and revolver and planned on padding my saddle bags with the inner juniper bark and dropping them to the earth below.

Again I thought of the snakes; I always had to think of the snakes because I couldn't ignore them, unless I wanted to die.

'Course, maybe I could feather them, though I didn't know how I would go about doing that. Feathered serpents had become a symbol of deadly power couched in affectionate behavior.

Maybe I could find some feathers, maybe not, but even if I had the feathers, would I want a snake affectionately curling around my body? Would my prejudice against one of God's creatures cloud my judgement? I needed to relax and trust in God. After all, God made the snakes, too—I think.

The sun came up bright, but in the west a storm was blowing. Clearly I wanted to work my way down Snake Draw before the rains came and filled the draw with water. I had charted my course in my mind, deciding not to go right down the sides of the draw where the snake population was so heavy. Rather, I would start at the top and walk down the water course to the mouth.

Bidding goodbye to Moroni's camp, it seemed that the pictographs also bade goodbye to me. Out of habit I cast my eyes around for She-Wolf, but of course she wasn't there. I followed the trail that led over the mountain to my water supply for water. When I was well onto the mountain, I cut over a low ridge covered with burro grass and sage and descended into the juniper that filled the head of Snake Draw.

The bottom of the draw was bare sandstone with pickets of sand. Making noise to warn the snakes as I walked, I took it slow and easy. On my shoulders and around my waist were all my earthly trappings, including my hundred-foot rope. But my hands contained nothing but my six-foot long snake stick with a Y on the end to pin the snake's head to the ground, should it come to that.

Not far to go, I suddenly saw a rattler making his way across the bottom of the draw twenty feet ahead. I paused, giving the reptile time to pass. As I waited, another snake appeared, traveling in the general direction as the first. Movement at my feet caught my attention and I glanced down at a rattler sliding over the toe of my boot. A shiver of fear zipped up my spine and I knew I was trembling in spite of all that I could do.

Sensing the tremor of my body, the rattler hesitated, testing

the air with his forked tongue. Willing myself not to make any
sudden movements with my feet, I brought my snake stick into
place, poised and ready to strike. I waited a long, tense moment,
my soul pleading a prayer to the maker of both man and reptile.

Who knows the mind of a snake? Surely not me. Yet for
whatever reason, the snake seemed satisfied and continued the
time-honored slither of his species, proceeding in the same
general direction as the other serpents. I breathed a sigh of relief
and looked for other snakes. The second rattler in front of me was
just disappearing among some rabbit brush up the side of the
draw. A quick search of the four directions told me there was a
snake behind me, but not close. One concluding glance to the
sides of the draw in front of me and I decided to make my move
while the way was clear.

When at last I reached the mouth of the draw, I was giddy with
relief. Within me was a surge of pleasure in my accomplishments.
There is no greater joy a man can feel than when he senses self
mastery, yet I couldn't help but wonder how much credit for my
success belonged to me and how much belonged to the Giver of
Life.

Rain clouds were gathering and far to the west I saw lightning.
Recalling that all the snakes I had seen were making their way in
the same general direction, I thought it possible that they sensed
rain and were seeking their den. Regardless, I hurried lest I would
have to wait out the storm before executing my escape.

Peering over the edge of the dry water fall, it was a drop of
maybe fifty foot or more to a pool in the wash below. I had already
descended an easy hundred foot or more and was on a level with
the top of the fan on either side of me. At this point the wash made
a bend next to the cliff to receive run off from Snake Draw and the
fan gave way to sheer cliffs. I was below the tips of the cottonwood
trees that lined the wash, but none of the trees were sufficiently
close to do me any good.

It seemed a long way down. For a moment a wave of fear,
almost panic, gripped my chest because I am not a real lover of

heights. Making the initial plans was one thing, but now that the moment of execution was at hand, I hesitated. Sinking to the rocks, I collected my wits and steeled my nerves as I endeavored to take control of myself as best I could. I was ready.

Tying my rifle and pistol to a long length of cordage, I lowered them. When they were almost to the water, I started them swinging like a pendulum. When they swung to the right, they touched the tips of cottonwood branches, but to the left they swung over dry sand. Timing my release, I released the cordage when the weapons were above the dry, sandy shores. Next I threw my saddle bags and they landed near the rifle and revolver. Then it was my turn.

Looping my rope around a juniper tree, I made both sides exactly even. They weren't long enough to reach the water below, but they came close.

Taking both sides of the rope in my hand at the same time for added strength, I cast a prayer toward heaven and started down, not allowing time for me to have second thoughts. A drop of rain (sweat?) touched my face.

Carefully I descended, inch by inch.

Something touched my back, ever so gently and I figured it was a bead of sweat sliding down. Again something touched my back and this time I was sure it wasn't sweat. I froze, fearful of what it might be. Was I getting jumpy? I screwed around to see the top leaves of a cottonwood branch. I let out a sigh of relief, chiding myself for getting all worked up over nothing.

I forced myself to relax and was beginning to feel good when suddenly something gave way and instantly my heart was in my throat. I felt myself shaking with fear, 'cause it felt like a tear in the rope. Again I felt the tear. The single rope held my weight when I pulled myself out of the chimney and I had the rope doubled, yet it was tearing. I had descended fifteen feet or less, with a thirty-five-foot drop. Should I climb back up?

The third time strands of the rope gave way and I could feel the sweat run down my face and drip off my chin. I was about to die and knew it; there wasn't a darn thing that I could do about it. Instantly my whole life seemed to pass across my mind, pausing on the incident weeks before when I lacked strength to pull myself from the chimney. It seemed that I was back in the chimney looking up into Moroni's face. "Have faith, Alma. The Lord hasn't forsaken you," he was saying, yet it wasn't faith that I needed—it was works.

Maybe I could have faith, I thought as my mind returned to the present. But maybe it was my time to die. Still, I closed my mind off to anything but faith. The leaf once more tickled my back and out of desperation I held to the rope with one hand and lashed out for the limb, drew the whole branch to me. I was trying to secure a hold on the thicker portion of the branch, yet the best I could do was to wrap my fingers around a portion of the branch that was no larger than my little finger.

There was no time to think because suddenly the rope gave way completely and I scrambled for more branches as I fell.

The tiny branch held for a minute, swinging nearer the main trunk of the tree, and I grabbed with my other hand for anything I could get a hold of. I grabbed something, but still I was falling. Before I knew it, I was splashing into the water below, precariously close to the edge of the pool and the base of the tree. In my hands was the huge cottonwood limb that had broken my fall.

I was free!

Life seemed good. Without any conscious thought on my part, I let out a yell of joy that would have scared a tired work-bull off his feeding grounds.

Swimming across the tiny pool to the side where my gear lay, I climbed out on the sand. The rain sprinkles were beating a steady rhythm now and to the west I saw more lightning. The skies were angry and the sounds of thunder rolled off the cliffs. Soon the wash would be running high with runoff.

Gathering my gear, I dashed across the wash and slid under a juniper. Because of the lightning, I didn't want to be under the towering cottonwoods, though I would have been drier. Resting with my back against the trunk, I munched on juniper berries and rabbit jerky as I watched. An inquiring trickle of water spilled out of Snake Draw, then suddenly, as if someone lifted an irrigation head gate, a full stream came, shooting twenty feet out into the wash.

I watched as the storm played itself out. Then the sun came out in all its glory, the earth steamed and the wash ran full. Like in the New Beginnings, an Indian celebration in many tribes, Earth Mother was in harmony, her body adorned with desert flowers and sweet smells. I wondered where She-Wolf was, but it didn't matter. She was free and so was I.

Gathering my feet under me, I studied the mountain above the cliffs. Maybe I was the only human to visit the mountain since Moroni, I thought, but then I remembered the skeleton. Still, I was free. After one final look, I turned my face toward the Crossing of the Fathers and eventually home.

I had traveled the length of time it took the sun to travel one hand in the sky and was climbing a low juniper-covered saddle. Always wary, I crept over a ridge and peered over before committing myself. What I saw brought me up short and set my heart pounding.

A riderless horse!

It wasn't a fancy animal, not by a darn sight, but an old sway-backed mustang. Not fifty feet away, the animal looked at me through curious eyes. Partly turned sidewise, the horse bore medicine man marking, but the crude saddle on its back was empty.

Holding my Winchester in my left hand, my right automatically dropped to the thong on my revolver, flipping it free of the hammer. Papa had always taught me to hold my rifle in my left hand when crossing hostile country, so that I could swing it quickly to the right. My right hand always stayed near my pistol so that I could quickly draw and shoot forward or to the left.

"*Maik'w* (hello)!" The salutation rang out sharply from my left and was designed to quickly capture my attention. Yet from long training, I cast my eyes to the right before turning them left, making sure it wasn't a trap.

At first I didn't see anyone, just a little color among the junipers. Then an old Indian stepped free of the greenery. Bow drawn, he had an arrow pointed toward my heart. The arrow had a flint arrowhead, rather than a fire-hardened wooden point. Dressed in a leather loin cloth and a poor-man's rabbit skin shirt that looked something like a scalp shirt, he just stood there with arrow poised. Iron cold eyes set in a leather face looked out at me from under a mountain lion cap that looked as old as the man himself.

Why didn't he release his arrow? Unless, of course, he wanted to save me for the squaws to torture. 'Course, all Indians don't torture prisoners, yet enough do that you just assume that if you are taken prisoner you will be tortured. There may be better reasons for capturing women or children, but not men. It's hard to make slaves out of most men and it is annoying trying to keep them from escaping, so men naturally assume the worst. With that assumption, you might do something foolish and get yourself killed, but under no circumstances would you allow yourself to be taken prisoner.

I don't remember drawing, but the next thing I remember was my .44 bucking in my right hand as I snapped my rifle up, shielding my heart. My bullet snapped the Indian's bow in two, probably because that was what I was looking at when I fired.

The Indian knew his stuff all right and his arrow flew true. Had I not snapped my rifle up over my heart, I would have been dead. Flint against steel sparked as the arrowhead struck the metal of my Winchester and shattered, burning me with hot sparks.

I stood there, pistol leveled at the Paiute. I expected the old man to dive for the relative safety of the junipers, but instead he slowly dropped his broken bow and ripped open his shirt, pointing to his heart. He was telling me to kill him quickly. I could see a reddening circle of blood on his upper arm where my bullet had gone after breaking his bow.

"*Kawtch* (no)," I muttered, returning my pistol to its holster. I knew he had not initially planned to release his arrow, or he would have done it from the safety of his hiding place before I reached the ridge. "Why did you ambush me?" I asked in Paiute. He looked perplexed, probably not understanding my words because of my white man or Shoshone accent, so I repeated them, slower.

"Me ambush you to talk," he replied, speaking the words slowly so that I could understand.

"With your arrow pointed at my heart it does not sound like friendly talk."

"Talk is friendlier when you have the advantage," he replied. "Little gun—magic."

I guess the Paiute had never seen a man draw and fire a revolver. Or maybe he didn't even know the pistol was there, as he was hiding on my left. He seemed to approve of my skill as fighting men appreciate skill, even in their enemies.

"Are you the Paiute that lives at the base of the cliff?" I asked. It was hard to read the Indian's expressions.

"*Aik'kookwai*," he replied in surprise. "My name is Posey."

"My name is Alma Harold," I replied, eyeing him curiously.

There was something strange about him that I couldn't place. He acknowledged my name but still I eyed him curiously, careful not to look directly into his eyes so that he wouldn't think I was rude.

"You are thinking that I don't look like a Paiute," he observed.

"Yes," I admitted.

"My mother was *Moo'keech* (Hopi)."

"Shall we bandage your wound?" I asked.

"*Ai'u whaihump* (it's all right)," he replied.

Still, we bandaged his wound and talked all afternoon. We talked slowly and as we did, I learned that some of the Paiute words that I learned from the Paiutes west of Manti were not the same as the words he used. Still, I was glad that Papa had insisted I learn sign language and several Indian dialects.

Deep in conversation, we stopped talking only when it got

dark. No need for a campfire, as we had nothing to cook, we settled down for the night about a hundred feet apart, as is the Indian custom when warriors are away from a village. I missed my fire because I didn't have a blanket. I was especially cold after the one o'clock chill set in, but I steeled myself against the cold and went back to sleep.

Something wet touched my face and I looked up into the eyes of a wolf. Startled, I strained to see the wounds left by the pygmy boar up on the mountain, She-Wolf's tell tale marks.

It was She-Wolf.

I drew her to me and spent the remainder of the night much warmer.

The new day dawned bright and warm. I hadn't seen Posey and had completed my morning devotional when I heard a low, guttural snarl from She-Wolf. Glancing up, I saw Posey standing, prayer stick in hand.

"*Toovuts*," he said, referring to the wolf in the sense of God.

"*Peah' suhnuv* (big coyote)," I corrected him. She-Wolf snarled and an attack seemed imminent to me.

"You best back up while I convince She-Wolf to go, Posey," I said in Paiute. "She is still a wild animal and I don't know how much I can control her."

Without reply, Posey extended his prayer stick in front of him and started chanting to the wolf. She seemed to relax a little, but slid close to me, almost as if she wanted me to protect her.

As Posey chanted he wasn't signing and I didn't know enough of the old Paiute language to know what he was saying. 'Course, some chants are just that—chants. The words sometimes come from an old language, the meaning long since lost to everyone but the shaman and sometimes even he doesn't know. I didn't interrupt because it was a conversation between the medicine man and She-Wolf.

Before Posey finished, She-Wolf turned and trotted the distance of a bow shot, then just stood there, watching us.

"You Wolf Man," Posey said. It was a statement, not a question.

"Wolf Man?" I questioned.

"Yes. You Wolf Man from the sacred mountain. You have great powers."

"The mountain may be sacred, but I don't have great powers. I just have the same powers as any other man. It's just that the female wolf was left alone and so was I. Wolves are social creatures that like to have their pack around. She simply adopted me, not wanting to be alone."

"Wolf Man has magic," Posey insisted.

"I can understand being called a wolf man, being that She-Wolf and I are friends, but I'm just a white-eyes that believes in the Great Spirit and not in magic." Paiutes do not refer to God as the Great Spirit, but I did, and knew Posey knew what I was talking about. They refer to their only real god and creator as *Toovuts*, a deity wolf, and *Soonung'wuv*, a mischievous legendary deity who was once human but became a coyote. Most western Native Americans think of the coyote as a trickster.

Don't get me wrong, the Paiute religion is fairly simple to understand. They do not worship the wolf or any other animal in animal form, they don't have a devil, they don't have as many superstitions as most tribes, but they believe in ghosts and evil spirits.

"How did you get off the sacred mountain?"

"It happened so fast I don't rightly know. I intended to climb down a rope, but the rope broke and mostly I fell from branch to branch down a cottonwood tree, then splashed into the pool where you get your drinking water."

"You make big medicine."

"What I call 'making medicine' is not the same as when you are making medicine. I worship the creator of the universe and call that power God or the Great Spirit."

"You observe the Great Silence."

"Yes. That's as good a time as any for morning prayer and better than most. What surprises me is that the Great Spirit is taking such good care of me when I'm such an ordinary person, not deserving any special treatment. More than once in the past two moons, I would have been dead if the Great Spirit hadn't been watching over me. But I don't have any magical powers."

"You crossed broken bridge. *Kwetoo'unuv* (master wolf) adopted you. You lowered sacred corn and a strange animal off Sacred Mountain for me to eat."

"The strange animal is only a pig. A *kwecheen'* (pig)!"

"You fell off cliff and were not hurt," Posey continued. "Little gun leaped into your hand."

"I understand it all except for the broken bridge. The bridge didn't crack until I put my weight on it."

"Bridge cracked when Posey has eleven summers. Posey's father cracked the bridge."

"*Uhmuh'ee mooum'* (your father)?"

"*Uh-uh* (yes). My father wanted to see the picture writing on sacred mountain. He crossed the stone bridge and the rock crack, so he couldn't return. Sacred mountain swallow him."

"You mean that I didn't crack the bridge by placing my weight on it?"

"That's right. My father cracked it. *Suhnuv* (another word for God) let you pass, but *Suhnuv* did not protect the Paiute warrior when he tried to pass. The mountain used to be a temple, but God turned the temple into stone when the people started doing bad. But on Sacred Mountain is a medicine rock for healing."

"How did you know about me crossing the bridge? Were you there?"

"I was not there, but I heard them talking about it."

"But there is nobody around for you to talk to."

"The village is not far away. I went to the village to show them the strange animal that you lowered in the basket from Sacred Mountain. I tell them of Wolf Man. They tell me of the bridge."

I glanced up at the top of the cliff a mile to the east, searching for Moroni's camp. Juniper trees hid the pictographs.

"You said that your father wanted to see the picture writing on the sacred mountain. How did your father know about the picture writings?" I asked. "You cannot see them because of the trees. Were the trees there when you were a boy?"

"I glimpsed the writing when I was a boy, before the tree grew as large as they are now, but when my father was a boy, he could see them. Father told Grandfather that he wanted to see them up close. Since then, trees continued to grow. Sacred mountain has hid them from all but you."

I nodded and he cast me a curious look that made me nervous.

"Wolf Man take Posey to picture writing?"

"Oh no, Posey. You have it wrong. I do not know how to get on top of the cliffs. You will recall that the natural bridge fell."

"Wolf Man will find way."

"*Posey, oonee' sump uk, oodoo'awvaw* (Posey, let it be, leave it the way it is)! *Nuh paiyuh'kwaivawnt* (I'm going home)!"

Posey studied something at his feet for a long time, saying nothing. After a while he said, "*Paiyuh'nait* (don't go home)."

"Posey, if there was a way to get up, you or someone else would have found it," I said in Paiute.

"It is death to go on the mountain unless you are with a man like Wolf Man."

"If it is death, why do you want to go up there?"

"Posey old man. I want to see picture writing before he dies."

"Still, I'm not going up there!"

We stood there in silence for a while and I recalled the Paiute skeleton on the lookout station. The skeleton must be the skeleton of Posey's father. Should I tell him about the skeleton? What would telling him accomplish? Maybe it would just heighten his determination to get me to take him up on the mountain. Yet I wasn't going back up there! No siree.

Glancing at the old man, I knew he would want to know about his father. Telling him would be the least I could do.

"There is a stone lodge near the top of the mountain," I began, "sort of a sentry station. In it is a skeleton of a man."

"One of the Old Ones?" he asked.

"No. I'd say the skeleton was fifty, maybe sixty years old. He still has a little leathered skin sticking to his bones and his dress is Paiute. On a table is a bow and quiver of arrows—Paiute arrows."

"It has to be my father. If it is, the arrows will bare his markings. I must go up there."

"I thought the Paiutes were afraid of the dead."

"Apaches and Navajos are afraid of the dead! Paiutes are not afraid of the dead! I just want to see the writings, but as long as I am there I want to see that my father's body bare the correct marking to help him cross the river."

"I don't understand. What markings and what river?"

"Father is a shaman, so his corpse should carry the markings of a shaman. When a Paiute dies, his spirit goes into the sky to a hole that all spirits have to pass through. After a while he comes to a large river, like the Colorado River, only larger. He has to leap over the river, but he can't unless he has pierced ears and markings on his body to help him get to his destination."

"But he has been dead a long time."

"That is true, but maybe his ghost is still waiting around for his body to be marked. Maybe his ghost helped you cross the rock bridge and jump off Sacred Mountain."

"Still, you would be walking with the ghosts of the dead."

"The young bucks in my village think that I am so old that I am one of the walking dead."

I grinned. The thought had crossed my mind, too.

"I do not think it would offend my father's spirit if I went up there and took care of his skeleton. Alma lead Posey up Sacred Mountain! Me see sacred writing. Me take care of father's skeleton."

"I am not going up there!" I snapped. "I told you that." Posey just stood there, thinking for a while before he spoke.

"Long ways to white-eyes village," he said, thoughtfully. "Long walk for Alma."

"*Kunuk'eunu* (what are you thinking about)?" I asked suspiciously.

"*Nuh'kuvaw voongkoo'kwunt* (I have a horse)."

"So?"

"Posey give Wolf Man horse if Wolf Man take Posey to pictures."

It was something to consider. I glanced at the sway-backed mustang, munching grass contentedly in a little depression down the ridge. It was a long way back to Manti and the sway-backed nag would help.

Mustangs are deceptive. They're more of a horse than most men give them credit for. Sure they are sway backed, but that's only because they are affectionate animals and allow the Indian boys to ride them while they are still colts. Their larger than normal heads give them an awkward appearance that white men often make light of. They're horses that can flourish on foods that other horses often won't consider, such as cottonwood bark, salt weed, greasewood, and creosote.

I glanced at Posey and he was looking out into space in the general direction of the sacred mountain. A hawk caught my attention, masked against a white pillow cloud. He was holding something in his talons, something tiny. Recalling the rattlesnakes the hawks caught on the mountain, I shuddered, my thoughts racing to Snake Draw and my escape.

I had an idea.

Turning to Posey I asked, "You did all right in calming She-Wolf. How are you at calming snakes? I understand that Paiutes do not care for snakes. But, of course, you are part Hopi."

He gave the white man's equivalent of a shrug. "Paiutes are not afraid of snakes," he said. "Wolves and snakes Posey understand." I had an idea that he could take care of himself around the snakes.

"*Oonee'umpawn* (I'll do it)," I said slowly.

## CHAPTER 8
# HOW TO DIE STANDIN' UP

I guess Posey had been gopherin' around these mountains and gullies since before Sittin' Bull was a calf. His hide seemed too leathery to wrinkle much and he was sometimes a little wobbly on his feet. I wondered how he could ever muster the strength to climb a cliff, but though I had only been with him for one week, I took him for a man that knew how to die standin' up.

To my way of thinking, the best way to return to Snake Draw was straight up the lowest point on the cliffs using a ladder. But can anyone make a ladder fifty feet tall, 'specially with only a stone tomahawk for a hatchet?

Surrounding the pool directly below Snake Draw were many tall cottonwood trees, some seventy-five or eighty feet tall. I had it in mind to topple one of them against the mouth of Snake Draw and use it as a ladder. Yet the base of the tree was nigh three feet in diameter, a formidable chopping project even for a white man's hatchet.

"Cut with fire," Posey suggested.

Cutting with fire was easier said than done. We built a small fire on the draw side of the tree and kept it going for days. It was good that we had plenty of water on hand, else we would have lost the tree on several occasions. Not that a blackened tree can't be used as a ladder, but we wanted to topple the tip of the tree into the draw fifty feet above.

We burned such a large hole out of the base of the tree that you would have thought the tree would fall over with only a slight pressure, but when we tried, it wouldn't budge. Then at night while we were asleep, a wind rose and the tree gave way, falling in the right direction. The next morning we found our ladder in place, maybe not exactly where we wanted to place it, but close enough.

Stuffing my flint into my pocket, I left my rifle and saddle bags at Posey's lodge, figuring that I could manage with only my Green River, pistol, and coffee pot. Posey gave me a sidewise glance but said nothing.

Climbing the cottonwood, I led out and Posey followed. When I reached the mouth of the draw, I stepped out on solid rock and prepared to hike to the top. Once we reached the draw, I had expected Posey to lead out, as he was the one that thought he could handle the snakes.

It had been a hard climb for the old man and he just stood there, catching his breath. But after a short rest, instead of continuing up the draw, he made a neat cache of his bow, quiver of arrows, and medicine pouch. Then he returned to the tree-ladder and started down.

"Aren't we going up the draw?" I said.

"We cross snake den at night," Posey replied.

"Why at night?"

"Nights are cold. Snakes go to lodges to cuddle." Why hadn't

I thought of that? When snakes are cold, they are drowsy and weak and less dangerous.

With Posey's cache, I deposited my coffee pot and cottonwood snake stick that I had painstakingly carved. Then I followed Posey back down the cottonwood tree.

Making several pitch torches, Posey sent me scrambling up the cottonwood to stash them with our cache, as we would be climbing Snake Draw at night and didn't want to climb up the stony spillway in the blackness. In case a rattler was spending the night under a scrub, we didn't want to rustle his lodge.

As I descended, I glanced at the cliff, then did a double-take. Amazed, I took time for closer scrutiny.

Handholds!

Yes, there were holes, chiseled into the stone as hand and foot holds. So that was how the original occupants of the mountain accessed it! Maybe they had toppled a tree at first, as we had done.

The holds had eroded over the centuries and didn't seem safe, but they were there. I didn't follow them all the way down to see if they were all intact, because we had the tree for a ladder and didn't need the holds. As soon as I got down, I told Posey about them and he was equally surprised.

Because I had lost my blanket to the Paiutes when my coyote dun went down, I slept under an overhang with a trench fire in front of me, the distance of a bow shot south of Posey's wickiup. When the one o'clock chill set in, I expected Posey to emerge from his lodge, but he didn't. Out of respect for his great age, I didn't press the medicine man, but put a little more wood on my fire and waited.

When at last the medicine man emerged, prayer stick in hand, he straightened to his full height, uttering a soft chant. In the starlight he looked more like a noble patriarch than the stooped old man he was. On his head were golden eagle feathers. Paiutes generally do not use bald eagle feathers as other tribes do because the bald eagle is a scavenger. Over his shoulders was a rabbit skin blanket.

Paiute rabbit skin blankets are different than you might think. They are woven, not sewn. The rabbit hide is cut in long strips about three-quarters of an inch wide and cut in a spiral, so you can have long strips from a small hide. The strips are wrapped over a long yucca string with the fur side out and twisted while the hide is still green. Then when it is time to make the blanket, they weave the rabbit skin strips with yucca string, much as the women back in Manti weave cloth. It makes a rectangular blanket the shape of a white woman's quilt.

"Wolf Man," he quietly called. I slid in beside him and he motioned that I was to lead out, saying something about my young eyes. We made our way to the cottonwood. There he removed his blanket and made a bundle out of it, then started his climb up the tree as I followed. In the stillness of the night I could hear his labored breathing. Several times he stopped to get his wind.

We were maybe fifteen feet up the cottonwood and Posey's breath was coming so short and ragged that I feared for him. Repeatedly he stopped and leaned against a limb for progressively longer periods of time.

"I'm an old man," he said when I cast him a questioning glance in the starlight, "but my heart is glad." At least I think that is what he said because his breathing was labored and his words were not clear. I eyed the limb that he was leaning on suspiciously and was about to say something because the limb looked too frail to hold him. It was dry with a split in it. But he was concentrating so much on his breathing that he wasn't paying proper attention to the limb.

Suddenly the limb snapped and Posey toppled forward into the blackness of space. I heard the solid sound of him striking sand below and the whoosh of his wind being pushed out of his lungs.

"Posey," I called, but of course he said nothing. You can't talk when the wind is pushed out of your lungs. Quickly I scampered down the tree, almost falling as I did. Posey was lying there in the shadows, struggling to get his wind. As quickly as I could, I gathered some inner bark and struck a spark. Then I added fuel for light and turned to Posey.

He didn't look good and right off I knew he had broken an arm because the end of a bone was protruding through the skin on his left forearm. But my biggest fear was that he might be paralyzed from the fall—I'd heard of such things. He was still struggling to get his wind and after a moment he moved his legs, which was a relief to me. At least he wasn't paralyzed—yet.

The only time to set a broken bone is within a few minutes of the accident, as the human body has a few minutes of relative numbness in which to work. After that few minutes, the pain sets in big time. So I took the old man's wrist in one hand and his elbow in the other and prepared to apply pressure and pull the bone back inside the skin. I glanced to Posey's face before I started pulling, wondering if he was ready. He set his jaw and nodded. I pulled.

"*Uddow'*," Posey said, nothing more.

As I increased pressure, the end of the bone was drawn under the surface of the skin. Then I gently released pressure, hoping that the ends of the bones connected. They seemed to have aligned up properly, so I nestled his arm in some slabs of cottonwood bark, putting the soft inner bark right in the wound to soak up the blood and tying it securely.

The rest of the night I sat beside the old man and when morning came, I went looking for some prickly pear and amarillo root. I made the prickly pear into a poultice to keep down inflammation and I boiled the amarillo roots, stirring the liquid into a foam for Posey to drink. I don't know what amarillo root does; it's just something medicine men always give you when you have been injured.

Posey grinned at me as I handed him the foaming liquid to drink. "Where you learn herbs?" he asked. "You medicine man?"

"My father's grandmother was a medicine woman," I replied. "She taught my father and my father taught me."

He nodded and drank the hot liquid.

"We go up on Sacred Mountain," Posey said when he had finished drinking.

"Posey!" I snapped in disbelief, "you aren't in any shape to climb up the cottonwood tree! Maybe it's even bad medicine." I wasn't sure that I believed the part about being bad medicine, but I thought Posey might.

The old man looked at me long and hard, then turned his intense gaze to the mountain itself. Clearly he was considering the situation. Then he turned his gaze back to me, with a determined set to his jaw.

"Posey go up Sacred Mountain to die," he said.

"Just how are you going to get up there?" I said in exasperation.

"Alma help me," he replied.

Well, there I had it. He was a determined old man that knew how to die standin' up. I had to admire him for that.

"But what if you are injured inside?"

"If I am injured inside, I will be just as injured up on Sacred Mountain as down here."

"All right," I replied, giving up on trying to talk him out of it. "But we will climb to the top of the cottonwood tree while it is still daylight. Then we can wait at the mouth of Snake Draw until you think it is safe to climb through the snake den."

Posey nodded.

That evening as the sun was setting, but still sharing light, Posey and I began the climb. We took it easy, limb by limb, step by step. And it was still daylight when we stepped onto solid rock atop the dry waterfall. Posey looked like death warmed over and almost fell to the rocks to rest. But as I said, he was a determined old man that knew how to die standin' up.

My first task on Sacred Mountain was to search for snakes. Then I struck a fire and we settled down to wait until Posey felt the time was right to hike up the draw.

As darkness took over, we moved closer to our fire. There was no moon, but overhead the sky was studded with a million stars. I glanced at Orion the Hunter, slightly visible over the eastern horizon. Orion seemed to smile as we started out.

Posey walked with his torch in his right hand, his hawk-feathered prayer stick resting gingerly in the fingers of his left hand. As he walked, he chanted a walking chant. You don't walk up to an Indian wickiup, tepee or hogan without hollering, "Hello, the hogan!" Likewise, according to Posey, you pay the same courtesy to the snake tribe.

We took it slowly, rock by rock, boulder by boulder. Painstakingly we skirted bushes and didn't see a single snake. Once we reached the top of the draw, I took the lead, making for Moroni's camp.

Circling the pictograph wall from the left, I descended into my old camp. The pictographs danced in the light of our torches as I gathered wood and lit a campfire. I wanted to settle in for another couple of hours sleep, as dawn was still a few hours away, but Posey added sagebrush to the fire. It didn't take much to realize that he was more interested in reading the picture writing than he was in sleeping.

As the sagebrush caught hold, it reflected off two eyes at the edge of the firelight, then the eyes were gone. Casting a sidelong glance at Posey, he was down on one knee with an arrow fit to his bow string.

"Maybe the eyes are from the ghost guarding the picture writings?" Posey offered.

"Maybe it's not a ghost but a wolf," I replied. "Maybe all the wolves on the mountain aren't dead."

Torch in left hand and .44 in right, I made my way to where we had seen the eyes, casting for prints.

Wild pig tracks!

"*Aik'kookwai!*" Posey said in surprise.

I felt a little sheepish, as the eyes of a pygmy pig are a lot smaller than the eyes of a wolf. Still, the little creatures were a formidable enemy.

"Sacred mountain has strange animals," Posey muttered.

"Uh-huh," I replied. Posey glanced at me 'cause "uh-huh" was not one of the English words he had learned.

"The wild boars did not come on this side of the mountain

when I was here," I explained.

"When you were here," he replied, "you had *peah' suhnuv* (big coyote). Maybe strange animals no like *peah' suhnuv*."

Morning came and Posey was at the wall reading the pictographs. Right off he pointed to the pictograph of the hunchback with the flute and said, "Posey know him. He Kokopelli."

"You mean you have seen similar pictographs of him before?"

"Yes, but I have also seen him. He came to our village once when I was a boy."

"How can that be?" I asked. "Aren't these pictographs hundreds of years old?"

"Yes, but Kokopelli has lived hundreds of years, too. Him go from village to village teaching people to plant the blue corn and live at peace with each other."

"You mean that he was here when Moroni was here?"

"Who Moroni?"

"Moroni is the lone figure seated at the table, writing."

Posey urged me to tell him what I knew of Moroni and of the white-skinned people that the pictures told of, so I talked the morning through, telling him. Even then the only reason why we moved was a desire for a drink of water. So in the high heat of the day we set off for the water hole.

I missed She-Wolf, yet my new companion, Posey, was even better. But I would be leaving him in a day or two, as I only agreed to take him to the pictographs in exchange for his old nag. Yet I was having reservations, because without his horse the old man would be stranded. Why was he out here anyway, miles from his village?

When we got to the water, it was cold and clear. I drank deeply and so did the old man. Satisfied, we entered the corn field, hoping to find some lingering ears. We found many, yet they were so old we considered letting them dry to grind them into meal.

For just an instant the odor of a campfire filled the air, then was gone. Glancing to the west, a ribbon of smoke floated to heaven.

"That looks like it is coming from Snake Draw," I said,

worried. "How could that be?" Yet we both knew how it could be and it didn't look good. Posey looked relaxed, but inside, my heart had sickened.

Sometimes when you burn a tree, a spark will remain long after you think it is out, especially when it is a big tree and it has been burning for many days. It's hard to chop the black away so as to make sure the fire is out, because if you had a good ax to chop with in the first place, you wouldn't have had to rely on burning the tree. Then, too, you can't pick up a cottonwood tree to make sure that its underside is fire-free.

A sickening feeling of impending doom gripped me with iron claws. Mentally, I kicked myself for getting into the fix I appeared to be in. I wanted to race to a view spot on the rim near Moroni's camp to see if the cottonwood tree was still leaning against the cliff. But Posey had it in mind to gather a shirt full of corn before we tramped back. He planned on grinding the corn for corn cakes.

What the heck, I thought, forcing myself to relax. We gathered the corn, which didn't take long and started back. Halfway to our camp, Posey spied a stone that would do dandy for a grinding stone, so he took my load from me, put it with his, and instructed me to carry the stone.

A hawk swooped, snatching a rabbit in its talons. "Hawk Brother," I grumbled, "why don't you catch the snakes and leave the rabbits for us." Posey glanced at me. Maybe he didn't understand all of my words, but he knew I was grouching.

"Bread better than rabbit," he said. Posey and I had been living on meat, so we both craved bread stuff.

Stopping at the camp only long enough to drop our load, we hurried to the rim of the cliff.

The tree was gone!

Falling to my knees, I buried my face in my hands in disappointment. My worst fears had been realized. I was numb with shock at what had happened, empty of thought. Posey just stood there, quietly sharing the same scene. Having once escaped from the jaws of the mountain, why did I allow myself to return?

Again I scanned the side of the cliff, 'cause the tree had to be somewhere. A lone tree the size of the cottonwood tree just doesn't burn all the way up. I detected a black streak across the water hole that looked much like a shadow cast by the long rays of the evening sun.

The cottonwood had fallen across the water hole! Even if I spent the weeks it took to make another rope, the blackened tree was directly below the mouth of Snake Draw. If I fell while descending, I would fall on the blackened tree remains and surely be killed.

While the sun descended the distance of two fingers in the west, I don't think I moved, 'cept to slap a pesky insect or two. When at last I glanced around, Posey was gone. No one wants to see a grown man cry, especially an Indian. Apparently he had left me to mourn our mutual fate alone. No one knew better than I the difficulty of escaping from the mountain.

Pulling myself together, I shuffled my way back to camp and found Posey busily working with the corn. Working as best he could with one hand, he kept the corn wet while he ground and as he collected enough of the wet grounds for a patty, he had me patty it into a corn cake, ready for cooking. When he tired of the one-hand grinding, I took over and the work went much faster.

"Tomorrow," he said as I approached, "we go hunting? We kill *kwecheen*'—has much fat for making corn cakes."

I nodded. Posey was certainly trying to help me forget my troubles and it was working.

The next morning I was preparing to move out for the proposed wild pig hunt, but Posey was puttering around among the junipers that grew between Moroni's camp and the rim of the cliff. When he returned to the camp, he had a dry sage limb in his hand. I was mighty curious, but it's easier to watch than to ask questions.

Catching the sage limb ablaze from the live embers from our fire pit, he dashed from tree to tree, lighting them. Completed, he watched the trees burn, his hands folded in content.

"Posey," I said, "what got into you? Why did you light the trees on fire?"

"Trees hide picture writing," he replied. "Posey wants grand-children to see pictures."

"I didn't know you had grandchildren."

"Posey old man. Have grandchildren."

"I understand. When you get off the mountain, you want to point out the picture writings to your grandchildren and tell them where you have been."

Posey cast me a long, thoughtful look, then for a minute he studied some red ants doing their ant thing. When he was ready to speak, he said, "Posey old man. Posey die on the mountain. Posey want Alma to tell grandchildren of the white Indians you call Nephites."

"You want me to bring grandchildren up on this mountain?"

"No," he replied. "Just point out the pictures to them."

There were long moments of silence cut by the noises of the insect tribe. From somewhere up the mountain a magpie scolded. A spark from the burning trees settled on my arm and I jumped.

"Well, let's get going," I drawled. "Them hogs are just awaiting for the slaughter." 'Course, Posey didn't catch all I said, but enough to know I was ready to turn my back on the heat of the burning trees and get on with our morning hunt. We hiked over the mountain to the water hole and tanked up on long drinks of water before beginning our hunt.

Though Posey was the senior, he took counsel from me on how to hunt the little beasts. "Pigs are smart," I said. "They're just about the smartest animal alive. You stand on the *rameumptom* and watch for movement, in case one of the little critters try to circle around behind me."

I started into an area of the corn field that I had never been in before, following the plan I had outlined. In my right hand my revolver was ready.

Of course the pigs could hear me coming and all I was likely to see were the feisty boars protecting their domain. The odds were unreasonable that Posey wouldn't see them before they attacked, but it gave him something to do, making him part of the hunt.

"Sun-wise," Posey yelled. Almost at the same time a vicious little boar came at me so fast that it was all I could do to snap a shot his direction. Too close to miss, the bullet pulled at the boar's body, but still he kept coming, teeth bared and mouth foamy. I snapped a second then third shot so close together that it sounded like one shot, but the little critter seemed immune to lead. By then the little beast was upon me. I met him with the toe of my boot and felt myself falling. I hit the ground hard, yet scrambled back up as best I could, for it seemed that my life depended on it. Some animals can do a lot of fighting even when hit in the heart. The grizzly bear that in 1806 mauled the famous mountain man Hugh Glass did all the damage to him after he had shot the bear through the heart.

On my feet I looked down at the boar, but the end had come for him. His torn body quivered and his blood was oozing into the vegetation. I nudged him with the toe of my boot, but he was dead.

It appeared that the report of my pistol shots broke the charge of other boar if indeed it was a charge. Scurrying sounds of the little animals fleeing through the undergrowth told us we could relax a little. I waited, making sure all the boars were gone, then slit the throat of our game. By then Posey was by my side and triumphantly we retraced our steps to the safety of the hillside, where we cleaned the game.

With thoughts of a special meal in mind, we hurried back to Moroni's camp to prepare our feast. After putting the pig in a pit to cook much the same way I had done weeks earlier, I watched as Posey went back to grinding corn. After a minute I pitched in and we worked together as we had done earlier.

I have never seen an Indian that couldn't eat more than a white man, because they are raised to gorge themselves when food is to be had, then fast when it is not available. That night I ate all the pig meat that I could, but Posey kept eating until the pig was gone.

We used the suet from the pig for corn cakes, adding a delightful flavor to the corn. Posey made a small canteen from the heart sacks of the pig. It didn't hold much, not even a full cup of water.

"Tomorrow," Posey said, "Alma take Posey to Father's skeleton."

"All right with me," I replied.

Too full to sleep well, I awoke well into the night, listening to the call of a lone wolf. Wondering if it was She-Wolf, I listened for an answering call, but heard none.

A hawk called as we prepared for the climb up the mountain to the rock lookout station the next morning. I glanced at the big bird, silhouetted against the only cloud in the sky and heard Posey say, "Good morning, hawk brother," extending his feathered prayer stick with his right hand. Again the hawk called and Posey replied, "We go to my father's skeleton." I glanced at the old man, bewildered. It was as if I were hearing one side of an intelligent conversation between an old man and a hawk.

We moved out, but Posey moved as if he could hardly walk. I glanced into his eyes, noting the strain in them.

"You are too sick to climb the mountain," I said. "Maybe we should wait until tomorrow."

"No," Posey replied. "We must climb mountain today!"

"Why today? I think you have internal problems from your fall."

"That is why we must climb today," he replied. His expression was that of determination, so there was nothing left for me to do but let him have his way.

We moved out slowly through the grass and rabbit brush. Posey began to do better at walking, but still he didn't seem to have the strength to chant to warn off the snakes, so I broke out in white men songs: "Yankee Doodle," "Turkey in the Straw," and the like. When we reached the steep portion, Posey was even slower and we rested often. Our progress was measured from step to shuffled step.

The climb took all morning and into the afternoon. How the

old man did it, I don't know. But he hung in there and kept moving, his breath coming short and ragged. Always he carried his prayer stick in his good hand. Occasionally I detected a faint chant for strength coming from his lips. I was beginning to understand some of his chants and songs.

Over the hill we hiked and as we descended to the lookout rock dugout, Posey seemed to gain a little strength. Fact is, the whole side of the mountain seemed to be filled with a sweet spirit, as if we had descended into a tabernacle. Into the clearing we hiked and Posey broke out into a different chant, extending his prayer stick.

At the ancient rawhide-covered door, Posey stood aside while I pushed it open and lit a torch for each of us. I poked my head in first to search for creepy crawlies, then stood back as the old man entered.

I followed the medicine man in and waited as he examined the arrows on the table. Handing his torch to me, I held both torches as he intensified his examination.

"Are they your father's?" I asked.

He nodded, a universal sign which the Indians probably learned from the white man, then he turned to the skeleton. I couldn't see what he was doing, except that he was putting marks on the body of some sort. After a while the torch grew low and I lit another, which I handed to him.

I stepped outside to give Posey a measure of privacy with his father and after a long time Posey joined me.

"Your father must have been a great shaman," I said.

"He was and he was an outstanding grandfather (teacher), too."

"What was his name?"

"We don't speak the name of the dead; you know that," he gently chided me.

"I thought you only never spoke the name of the dead when you didn't want their ghost to haunt you."

"That is true. The purpose of not speaking the name of the

dead is so that we won't summon his ghost."

There was a long moment of silence. Then Posey slowly said, "*Oong'wai neum Taioo'soov* (his name is Whittled Stick)."

Immediately a gust of wind seemed to appear from nowhere like a tiny whirl wind. It caught the door that was standing open and violently blew it closed, then it zipped across the face of the mountain.

"Father is here," Posey grinned.

"This is a good place to camp," I observed aloud after we had traveled a few hundred feet.

"I feel strong enough to return to Moroni's camp," he replied. I nodded and noted that he seemed to have gained a little strength by the rest, while he was doing whatever-he-was-doing with his father's skeleton. He was even beginning to take regular steps, rather than shuffle. Of course we were going down hill.

"The visit to your father's tomb lifted your spirits," I observed aloud.

"The village always wondered what happened to him," Posey replied. "I dreamed that I would see him one last time before I died."

Indians highly regard dreams—maybe too much, to my way of thinking. When they feel like being close to the spirit, they put on "strong medicine," which means they put on the things they saw in their dreams—feathers, claws, small bones, small pieces of dung, whatever they have dreamed that represented great powers. Still, dreams are also spoken of in a very favorable light in the Bible.

A happy old man walked back to Moroni's camp and I was happy because he was happy.

Back at the camp, Posey gathered ashes from the juniper trees and scattered them liberally around our sleeping area.

Seeing the curiosity in my expression, he asked, "Don't White Eyes circle their beds with ashes in snake country?"

"I never heard of it."

"Snakes do not like to crawl over ashes."

"Makes sense," I muttered, "but it beats me why there are so many snakes on this mountain. How'd they get here?"

"They flew."

"Snakes don't fly! Everyone knows that."

"Yes, but they used to fly. They had wings at one time."

"Is that *tookwee'nup* or *nawduk'gwenup*?" I asked. A *tookwee'nup* is a winter story or legend, a humorous story with a moral meaning, but more or less a fairy tale. A *nawduk'gwenup* is a true story from Paiute history.

"It's *nawduk'gwenup*," he replied

Well, I let that pass. I didn't believe that snakes ever had wings. We went to bed and in the middle of the night I awoke, thinking about snakes with wings. Seems that I remembered something from the Bible about flying serpents, or was I just dreaming?

The nights were cold, but the days were hot. As the birds woke us the next morning, the skies were studded with stars and I knew it was going to be a hot day. When Posey folded up his rabbit-skin blanket, he handed it to me.

"*Oodoo'unum* (yours)," he said.

"Mine? I can't take that! You need it!"

"Posey need it no more," he replied, turning on his heels.

"Posey—" I started to protest, but he had turned his attention to other things. Oh well, I thought. I will speak with him about it tonight.

The sun was two hands high in the sky when we made our daily trek to the water tanks. I hadn't broached the subject of our escape from the mountain because I doubted that Posey had any answers. Still I had thought of it often, racking my brains for any morsel of knowledge that might help. The handholds I had seen while descending the cottonwood tree were worth investigating, but in order to investigate them we would have to pick our way down Snake Draw.

I had been away from Manti all summer and there was a longing in me to go home. I made up my mind to climb down the handholds, or attempt to. If they didn't go all the way, I'd just climb back up and try something else.

"Posey," I said as we rounded the mountain and were about to descend to the water hole, "tonight I go down Snake Draw."

Posey grunted but said nothing.

"Are you going with me?" I asked.

He merely grunted again.

"Posey, I'm going to my home in the white man's village of Manti and I'm not gonna take your horse. You can't leave this mountain with your broken arm, but when it heals you will want to climb down and go home. You will need your horse." I knew that the horse was the trade we had agreed upon when I consented to guide him, but if I took the horse he would be stranded. The nag was corralled in a green valley on the flood plains of the wash, below and to the south of Snake Draw.

Posey still hadn't said anything, though he had listened intently.

When we reached the water hole, Posey took a long drink, then continued to the *rameumptom*, where he sat cross legged, singing. Most white men can't tell singing from other chants and I can't say that I always can, either. But it sounded like the songs Billy use to sing when he sang the songs of his childhood among the Shoshone.

As the hours passed, I lay on my back listening to the soft chants drift across the mountain and watched the clouds. Now that my decision had been made, climbing down the cliff didn't seem so drastic. Sure I didn't care for heights, but I could steel myself against fear. After a while I set to work making several torches I'd need for walking down Snake Draw at night.

Gradually I realized that Posey had stopped his chanting. Glancing in his direction, I saw him just quietly sitting, meditating. All day he sat there and it was about time to leave for camp, to cross the mountain trail before dark.

Making my way to the *rameumptom*, I hailed, "Posey! We go!" He didn't say anything. He just stared into his lap.

"Posey, we go!" I called again.

He lifted his tired eyes to mine and attempted to raise his prayer stick. Something was wrong.

Climbing the *rameumptom*, I knelt beside him. Too weak to talk clearly, he muttered something in Paiute. As near as I could tell he had said, "Show Posey's grandchildren the pictures that talk."

"Your people chased me last time I went to the village and tried to kill me," I accused. "They might try again."

"Trust in *Toovuts* and the ghosts of the dead," he said. "Maybe even I will be one of the ghosts. And take my prayer stick so they know I sent you."

He said no more, but seemed to be having a hard time breathing. His left hand went to his chest and he tensed, as if he were in pain. Beads of sweat broke out on his forehead. Trying to make him comfortable, I laid him on his side, though his feet hung over the edge of the *rameumptom*. Starring into space, he whispered, "*Taioo'soov*," the name of his shaman father. A breeze rustled the stocks of corn, as if his father's ghost was answering him.

"Don't die," I whispered.

But he did.

Again, I was alone.

# CHAPTER 9
# THE MOUNTAIN KNOWS NO MERCY

The mountain knows no mercy, has no feelings. Yet I was alone, just me and the cold hard mountain.

Reverently I carried Posey's body to the side of the mountain, not far from the water hole. Kindling a fire, I sat beside him all night. I wished for She-Wolf and once during the night heard the mournful call of a lone wolf from the west. Again I listened for an answering call and this time heard an answer from the north. Had She-Wolf found herself a new pack?

The next morning I made a tomb out of an overhang and reverently slid Posey's body inside on his back facing east, Paiute style. On my knees I thanked Heavenly Father for Posey's friendship. Posey had released She-Wolf when I lowered her from the cliff. Later, his enthralled interest in Moroni's picture writing as I rehearsed to him the stories of the Nephite destruction had surprised me. Again I was surprised at his gentle concern when I was distraught over the cottonwood tree ladder burning to the ground.

I walled up the front of the overhang with stones, giving Posey's body a measure of security from the elements, enclosing all the worldly possession he had with him when he died, except his prayer stick, as he had directed. Then I trudged back to Moroni's camp, prayer stick in hand.

Though I had not really known Posey long, the camp seemed to remind me of him. There were a few corn cakes left and I recalled how he and I had made the corn cakes together. Was everything I saw going to remind me of him?

The camp looked quite different with the trees gone. A few black stumps remained, which I pulled down so that Posey's wish of allowing his grandchildren to see the pictographs could be realized. Posey had also asked that I tell his children of the picture writings, but I wasn't sure I wanted to do that.

Neatly placed on a sandstone near where Posey had slept was his blanket, his gift to me. Surely he knew he was going to die. Maybe he willed himself to die. I had heard of such things. Native Americans are close to nature and spiritual matters, regardless of which Native American religion their tribe clings to.

All day I lounged around camp and prepared myself for the middle of the night when the snakes would be cold and groggy.

The deep chill of the night had set in when I woke from a fretful sleep. It was warm under Posey's blanket, so I would have slept well were I not so concerned about walking down Snake Draw. I had planned on waiting a few hours longer before I arose, but I couldn't sleep. So I arose, bundled up my trappings, and made my way to the head of Snake Draw.

The thoughts of descending into the draw made me about as uncomfortable as a horse thief at a hangin' bee. I lit a torch so that I could see, then took a big breath to calm myself. After casting one final prayer toward heaven, I started down, taking it mighty easy.

I didn't know any chants like Posey had sung while coming up the draw, nor did I feel like singing. But I needed to warn the snakes of my intrusion, so I filled my lungs and sang "They're Tenting Tonight On the Old Camp Grounds." The song did more than warn the snakes; it relaxed me, sending a calmness into my soul that surprised me, a calmness that I hadn't felt before in snake country. Still, I took it easy, one step at a time and skirted all the bushes.

The flicker of the torch casts its own shadows in the night, shadows that moved as I moved. The night was cool with a low breeze coming from the south, yet I was sweating. Surely the snakes were cuddling in their lodges on such a cool night, the way Posey had predicted.

The breeze raised some dust and flickered my torch. Then I heard it. A rattle from my left, followed by a rattle from directly behind me. Maybe I should have jumped, but instead I froze, peering into the darkness. The flickering light from my torch danced on dry seed pods, rattling in the breeze. I suddenly became aware that I had palmed my revolver.

Wiping the cold sweat from my forehead, I struggled to regain composure. Why was it so much easier for me to face a man with a gun than to face a snake in the darkness? Steeling my nerves against the unknown, I regained my composure to some degree and started moving again, placing each foot carefully, mindful not to step into dark spots. Often I stopped to listen to the sounds of the night. I must continue to sing, I thought, and started afresh singing "They're Tenting Tonight on the Old Camp Grounds."

The stars had moved less than two hands in the night sky when I reached the mouth of the draw and surprisingly I hadn't encountered any snakes. Overhead, Orion the Hunter kept watch. Even with him watching, the darkness of night was no time to locate foot and hand holes on the cliff, so I settled down for the rest of the night.

It was cold. Though still August, the chill of autumn was in the air. I had Posey's blanket, though I still wanted a fire. There was no sign of snakes at the mouth of the draw, so I figured that by probing first with my snake stick, I could safely collect enough wood for a fire. So carefully—so very carefully—I collected firewood and lit a fire on the edge of the dry waterfall.

The birds signaled the approaching dawn and as the skies grew light the Great Silence came and went, but the sun was still hid behind the mass of the mountain to the east. Carefully I searched for the foot holes and hand holes, becoming frustrated at my inability to locate them. When at last I found them, they were on the north side of the dry water fall, connecting about twenty feet up from the base of the draw. Giving one final prayer, I steeled my nerves and tried to relax. Then I started down.

For several feet I climbed straight down, but then I couldn't find a hole for my foot. Timidly I glanced below my right foot, but couldn't see a hole at all. Then I looked below my left foot and saw that the trail moved to the left a little.

I was about forty feet above the edge of the pool and directly under me was the blackened cottonwood stump. This was the level where I had seen the holes while descending the cottonwood days earlier. Fifty feet to my left and maybe two hundred feet to my right were the tops of the debris fan. But directly below Snake Draw the debris fan gave way to a bend in the wash, which moved in next to the cliff.

Another five steps and once again I couldn't find the foot holes. Glancing below my lower right foot, I couldn't see any holes. Scanning the cliff to my left I still didn't see any holes. Puzzled I looked again, then noticed that a large section of stone had broken away. Casting a prayer toward heaven, it occurred to me to look for the hand holes.

The hand holes went directly north, but where the foot holes should have been, a section of the cliff had broken away. Straining for a better view, I saw the foot holes beyond the broken portion, about six feet north. Could I cross using the hand holes only...for six feet? The answer was clearly no! The holes were weatherbeaten and my feet would be dangling in space. I started back and realized that my muscles were trembling. I must calm myself.

For a few seconds I cowered against the side of the cliff, willing myself not to tremble. I must have faith in myself, I thought. I recalled the words of my mother saying that without faith in one's self, one can't have faith in God. Odd that I should think of that at a time like this. Of course my mother was right; everything she ever told me was correct.

"I can do it," I said aloud. "I can do it. I can do it." I knew I could do it if I were only two feet off the ground, but I was much higher. There, hanging from the cliff, I closed my eyes and said a prayer, pleading for strength to climb back up.

"Don't climb up," a soft voice spoke. "Climb down." I glanced both directions, but I didn't see anything. Was Posey's ghost speaking to me?

"I can't climb down," I replied aloud to thin air. "I cannot dangle high above the ground by handholds only." Even as I said it, it occurred to me that I could climb by the handholds if I were only two feet above the ground. Maybe I could do it. After all, it wouldn't take any more muscles to move side-wise, hand-over-hand by using the handholds only than it would to climb back up the face of the cliff.

Changing direction, I worked my way back to the section of cliff where the surface had fallen away. I took several deep breaths, relaxed my muscles as best I could, then reached for the hole to my left. Obtaining it, I moved my right hand into the same hole. Sliding my feet out of the final foot hole, they dangled as I hung on with my right hand and reached left for another hole. Finding the hole I started to release my right hand, with the intentions of hanging by the finger of my left hand, but suddenly my left hand started to slip as the surface of the stone loosened.

"Jesus," I cried. "Save me!"

"I am here, Alma," a voice spoke. It wasn't Posey's voice, but a soft, calm voice that spoke in perfect English. "Let go with your right hand and I will support you."

There comes a time in life when you just have to trust someone or something, and that time had come for me. So I let go with my right hand and instantly I realized that my foot was resting on something spongy. I gave it my full weight and it held. Placing my right fingers in the same hold as my left, I wiped out the loose material with the finger tips of one hand. I glanced down to see what I was standing on. There was nothing there, just thin air.

"Move on," the voice said, and I obeyed. I reached for the handhold on my left, swinging in order to reach it. Having obtained the hole, I cleaned out the hole with my index finger while holding on with the other fingers. Several grains of material came loose. Satisfied, I committed my weight to the hand hole, then let go with my right hand. As I did so, my spongy footing held. What was I standing on? Was I literally being held in the hands of Jesus?

A third, fourth, and fifth time I repeated the process, but on the sixth time I couldn't find the hole. Returning to my fifth hole, I studied the wall. One hole was missing. Could I stretch to the seventh hole?

"Lean against the wall," a voice said. "You are in my hands, and I won't let you down."

I held on with my right hand and leaned against the wall as I reached past the missing handhold to the seventh handhold. It was about a thirty-inch reach, but I made it. Catching the hole with the tips of my fingers, I worked my fingers into it, then to the far side so that I'd have room for both hands. Carefully I released my right hand and brought both hands together in the hole. I felt a surge of accomplishment.

While reaching for the next hole, my foot slid into a foot hole and the spongy foot hold was gone. I realized I had crossed the difficult section. "Thanks, Jesus," I muttered as I moved along the cliff for several more feet, I allowed myself a moment to take a breather. Glancing down, I realized I was only thirty feet above the debris fan—still a long way, but relatively close.

Two more holes and my probing fingers closed on grass and tiny twigs, some bird nest of a sort. Cleaning out the hole, I continued, the sense of accomplishment growing.

My feet struck solid debris before I realized it. I stepped back from the cliff on the debris fan, wobbling a little and sat down, almost falling to the rocky slope. A great load had been lifted from my shoulders both mentally and physically and I felt totally drained, yet giddy with joy as I sank to my knees to thank Jesus for sparing my life.

A black wasp with orange wings whisked past. Maybe this isn't a good place to relax, I thought, because I am not one that likes to share his space with wasps. Rising to my feet I almost stepped on a tarantula, a three-inch black furry spider. Made sense, I thought, because I have heard tell that the wasps with the orange wings have to have tarantulas to survive. Billy, who knows a heck of a lot more about the insect tribe than me, said the wasps kill the tarantulas, lay their eggs in their bodies, then bury them.

Gingerly I picked my way down the fan to the water hole for a long drink of life-giving fluid. Then I stepped back, studying the cliff and the route I had come.

Life seemed good.

# CHAPTER 10
# A QUARRELSOME BREEZE

The base of the cliff was a land best suited for scorpions and horny toads. A quarrelsome breeze stirred the dust as I dragged my tired frame through a patch of sore-eye poppies, skirting a giant prickly pear that was growing into the branches of a scrawny juniper. A lizard zipped out from under the cactus to a sandstone slab and studied me whimsically. Giving him only a passing glance, I trudged on to Posey's wickiup where I had cached my rifle and gear.

My mind kept wandering to Posey's request for me to show the pictographs to his grandchildren. One time he said his son was named Red Coal and was a medicine man like himself. But he hadn't told me the names of his grandchildren nor where they lived, though I supposed they were in the Paiute village to the east, beyond the sacred mountain.

Visiting the village was not something I wanted to do, yet I had the nagging feeling I owed it to Posey. It seemed there were too many ponderables, too many intangibles, too many unknown things for me to foresee what I should do. I'd just have to rely on the Great Spirit or Jesus, whatever you call him. Of late I had felt the Great Spirit's presence and had faith he would see me through.

I walked the final steps to Posey's wickiup and collected my gear. Then I crossed the wash and turned my face and feet south, toward the little valley where Posey's mustang was secured.

The horse nickered as I approached, yet she looked past me, expecting Posey. I talked to her, patting her neck and withers, and she accepted the attention. On her hip were medicine man markings, painted and repainted so many times the old nag was almost tattooed. Though I would try to remove them, chances were she would carry traces of them until the day she died.

From Posey's nearby cache I retrieved his saddle blanket and Paiute saddle. Contrary to the opinion of many white folks, most Indians that spend much time on a horse use a saddle, or at least a folded blanket; young bucks or warriors in battle are the exception.

Saddling up, I wiled away the rest of the day, just a man and his horse, getting acquainted. When a man has to depend on an animal, he naturally wants to know what it can do. And the horse seemed to like the workout.

The sun was two hands high when I returned to the little valley. Stripping the saddle and blanket from the mustang, I rubbed him down with dry grass. The horse rolled, then took to cropping grass as I busied myself making stirrups for Posey's saddle, using cordage from yucca fibers. That night I bedded down near my horse.

Totally worn out, the last thing I remembered before falling asleep was the call of a night hawk and the low wind whispering through the junipers and around the rocky ledges.

The mustang awoke me. She was nervously listening to

something moving, up in the trees. Mustang horses, bred to the wild, are better watch dogs than most dogs.

Repeatedly she sniffed for a scent. Clearly she didn't like what was out there. I thought of the night hawk I had heard earlier and wondered if it was a real hawk, or the Paiutes signaling to each other.

Rifle in hand, I slid into the deep shadows of a juniper. I slid the thong off my pistol and waited. The horse snorted, pawing the ground with her hooves. It occurred to me that if it were Indians out there, the horse wouldn't be so nervous, being that she was an Indian pony.

The shadows cast by the moon were long and deep. But as I watched, something slid from one shadow to the next.

"She-Wolf," I softly called. In the darkness I couldn't tell one wolf from the next, but She-Wolf came to me, squirming and letting her tail wag her body. The mustang went wild, head down and snorting.

I stroked She-Wolf's silver-gray coat affectionately and she licked my arm. Then I heard something in the shadows. Glancing over her shoulder I saw other wolves, maybe forty feet distant.

Quick as I could, I struck a spark into a nest of inner juniper bark. She-Wolf was okay, but I didn't know about her newly found pack. She had been with me long enough that she was accustomed to fire, so she didn't run when I struck the spark. Soon as I had the nest burning, I added wood, then some dry sagebrush for high flames. The pack pulled back and the mustang settled down somewhat, though she clearly didn't like sharing her night with She-Wolf.

It was light when I was nudged awake by the mustang. She-Wolf was gone, as were the other wolves of her pack. I threw a little water on my face, then plopped several juniper berries into my mouth to clean my teeth. Going to Mustang, as I named my horse, I spoke softly and patted her. She might have been a little sway backed, but she was a horse to stand beside a man and she liked affection.

In my mind was a determination to get it over with, to go to the Paiute village and deliver Posey's dying message. So I slipped into my buckskin shirt, as I don't like to wear a linen shirt when visiting an Indian village. It never pays to flaunt something others want and Indians seem to like the colorful calico linen shirts I wear. The morning air was cool, so the leather shirt felt good.

When my mother makes buckskin shirts, having been taught by Papa, she puts the thickest section of the buckskin on the front panel of the shirt. You have to use the thick parts of the hide someplace and the front is the best place because it is useful there for warmth. When riding you create wind that drains the heat from your body mass, but if your chest is shielded by thick buckskin to cut the wind, you're warmer. The bad part of it is that the front is too thick for needles to penetrate easily, even steel needles like white folks use. So the front of your shirt goes undecorated.

As long as I wasn't wearing my linen shirt, I washed it and placed it on my chest next to my skin. I have found that the best place for a traveling man on horseback to dry a shirt. If I just wore the shirt in the open to dry, it would get dirtier than when he started, because horseback riding is a dusty business.

Saddling up, I tied my saddle bags and bulky blanket roll behind the saddle and slid my toes into my newly created stirrups. The saddle didn't have a scabbard for my rifle, so I used a strip of cordage to sling the rifle over my back like a quiver of arrows.

Sitting tall in the saddle, I turned Mustang's head toward the village. The horse seemed to know where to go. I didn't know exactly what I would do when I got there, but I wanted to get well inside the village before being stopped. Though I wasn't familiar with Suhuh'vawdutseng Paiute customs, in most tribes a man is safe within the village and is treated as a guest. It's before he reaches the village and after he leaves that he is most vulnerable, as he no longer falls under the protective umbrella of the village. Still, I wasn't sure, because all tribes, indeed all villages, are different. I recalled that I had almost reached the village once while riding my coyote dun and had been accosted by a bunch of young bucks. I had found them to be quarrelsome rowdies, no less. I had been lucky to escape with my life! I shuddered. Was I on a fool's errand? As Posey advised, I needed to rely on God.

Death seemed to ride the dry hills and it seemed a haunted place. The sun floated in the heat-glazed sky, trying to beat some sense into me. I found myself letting the horse pick the way, as she knew Posey's route. The animal chose to go straight up a hill that was so steep only a mountain goat or a mountain-bred mustang could make it.

Catching a view of the village from a ridge, I reigned in and set the horse, getting a good feel for the village. Made up of three to four dozen wickiups and one tepee, the village seemed to lay quiet in the morning sun. Occasionally a naked child could be seen at play. At the far end of the village several boys were wrestling Indian style. Indian style wrestling is stand-up wrestling. The boys can use their feet, head, or anything but their hands. Hands are traditionally reserved for holding weapons, which is why Indians are so amazed at white men's use of fists. When the boys had enough, they would sit or lie down, by that act conceding defeat.

The Paiutes, at least the Paiutes in Utah, are generally an easy-going people. They eat what comes along and live where the food they like is found. Some are elk and deer eaters, some rabbit eaters, and some insect eaters. There are tribes, such as the Apache Tribe, that don't eat certain foods like fish or snakes or birds and the list goes on and on. But the Paiutes eat everything and that in itself brings condemnation upon them from other tribes such as the Apaches, Navajos, and Arapahos.

They live and sleep almost anywhere, also. They make brush wickiups, or maybe just sleep under a bush with a hide thrown over the top. Sometimes they make tepees and when they do, they make them out of elk hides. The elk hides are stretched so tightly over the tepee poles that they don't get hard when they get wet from the rains.

They are a handsome people, and when you are around their

tepees you will notice that they do not smell offensively, as do some Plains Indian tepees that use urine-tanned buffalo hides. Generally their tanning substance is boiled brains. They sometimes use sweat lodges, but they are for cleanliness. No religious significance is attached.

They are not an agricultural people, but do like corn. Therefore some of them grow small fields of corn and occasionally squash and melons. They also usually get along with non-Paiutes, but as I had learned earlier, when they get riled up they are hell on wheels.

Studying the village, I saw that to one side was a herd of a dozen horses, small compared to the size of the village. Paiutes love horse meat, so even if they don't ride they keep horses around. All the signs I had seen thus far told of a poor village that relied heavily on small game for food. Posey had been wearing a rabbit skin shirt rather than buckskin.

Taking time to remove my pistol and holster, I rolled them into my blanket and tied it securely. I didn't want to ride into the village exhibiting too many of the things an Indian might want. It was enough that my rifle could be seen.

I nudged Mustang out. She knew where to go. With experienced hooves, she picked her way down a narrow arroyo unseen from the village. My guess was that Posey didn't like to advertise his comings and goings, so he entered and left by a back way. Most Paiute villages return to the same camping spots each year, following the game. Still, the tepee told of added stability to the village.

Coming out of the arroyo, Mustang picked her way along a ribbon of a path, nestled between the steep slope of the mountain and several Paiute garden plots. Growing in the gardens were clumps of corn, beans, pumpkins and in the distance I thought I recognized the huge leaves of watermelon plants. The crops looked good but pitifully few for a whole village.

A Paiute woman, working in her garden, raised her head and studied me mutely. She was wearing a cone-shaped hat and on her feet were yucca slippers. All of the Paiutes that I ever knew either went bare footed or wore badger moccasins in the summer and yucca slippers covered with rabbit fur in the winter, but maybe the slippers were left over from last winter. I nodded at her, wondering if she would nod back. She didn't.

I passed a sweat lodge. Decisively Navajo in appearance, it looked like a miniature hogan.

I don't think it is possible to enter an Indian village unseen in broad day light, so I am sure that sentries had sounded the alarm long before I reached the first wickiup, though there still wasn't much movement. Dogs barked and naked children gawked as Mustang moseyed along. I wondered how I would find Posey's kin. 'Course, most likely the whole village was his kin.

To my left I passed the tepee. It carried the markings of a shaman and looked out of place in the brush village. I wondered if it was Red Coal's lodge, though Posey hadn't said his son was a shaman. He had said his son was a medicine man. 'Course, a shaman is a medicine man, but a medicine man who deals more with the religion. He is not someone to be taken lightly. Some rival the prophets of the Old Testament for personal purity, but others are into black magic. Though Posey was a very spiritual man, he seemed more interested in herbs and was something of an Indian scholar, if there is such a thing.

Glancing at a fox pup, I looked again. My brother Billy told of having a fox for a pet when he was a boy living with his Shoshone family. Indian children make pets of almost anything, or try to. As I rode on, I saw a badger that was watching several children at play. When trained, badgers follow Indian children around much as a dog might, but this badger was intently watching the children play *tawsuhng'uhmp*, the rabbit skull game, and trying to get into the act. The game is played by tying a short piece of yucca cord to a rabbit skull, leaving a foot of slack, then tying the other end of the cord to a pointed bone. Then the child tosses the skull into the air and tries to get one of the holes in the skull to land on the pointed bone.

On her own volition, Mustang stopped in front of a nonde-script brush wickiup, as if she had been there many times before. Children crowded around, gawking but almost mute. A short man stepped out, ducking to clear the brush. When he straightened to his full height I thought I was looking into the eyes of Posey, 'cept the eyes I was looking into were much younger and maybe a little harder.

Holding Posey's prayer stick in my left hand, I kept my right near my rifle and waited for an invitation to dismount. But he just stood there, studying me and the horse, not extending the invitation.

"You Posey's son?" I asked. I thought that would be better than if I asked for Red Coal by name.

"I am," he replied, clearly a little surprised. "I am Red Coal." Mulling his name in my mind, I wondered how he got it.

"My name is Alma. Your father sent me. Said to give you this prayer stick as a sign that he sent me." I offered him the prayer stick, but he didn't accept it or even move. He just stood there. This visit didn't seem to be going so well.

"Posey was my friend," I said. "He has gone into the hole in the sky and has crossed the great river. Before he died, he gave me a message for his grandchildren." At that, Red Coal seemed to raise his eyebrows a little.

"Dismount and we will talk," he said.

Just then a loud voice barked from behind. Turning I saw a large, fairly handsome young Paiute atop a mustang stallion, sitting proud as a peacock in *my saddle*! I had seen him before. He was one of the Paiute rowdies that had accosted me months earlier. A trickle of sweat made its way down my spine.

Jabbering to me in Paiute, he was talking far too fast for me to grasp any words, though they were obviously fightin' words. Throwing his left foot over his mount's withers, he dropped to the ground, drawing a flint knife in one fluid move. Apparently I was being challenged.

"Is this the way Paiutes treat guests?" I said to Red Coal using a mocking tone quality to my words.

"Him Pook, son of the shaman. Shaman also war chief. No one tells him how to act," came the reply.

It made sense, I thought. In most—maybe all—Indian cultures, war is a religious experience. The young warrior gets an idea, maybe dreams a dream of conquest, or sees a vision in the smoke of the ceremonial fire and the idea takes in all the fervor of a protestant revival. Yet he generally will still want to go to the shaman and get him to seek a religious sign.

"Did your shaman," I said on a hunch, "come from one of the Paiute bands west of the Colorado River?"

"Him come from the west," Red Coal replied. It was just as I thought. The shaman and war chief was probably a disgruntled refugee from Black Hawk's fighting band. Again Pook shouted an angry challenge and once again he spoke far too rapidly for me to understand. The farther south you get in Paiute country, the faster they talk. They say that the Paiutes in Las Vegas talk so rapidly that the northern bands can't understand them.

"Tell Pook him baby wolf with big bark," I said softly. Red Coal looked uncertain, but delivered the message. The meaning was not lost on Pook nor the crowd that had gathered. Baby wolves bark and yip a lot, much like domestic dogs. Adult wolves don't bark at all, because somewhere in adolescence the adult wolves teach them not to bark.

A murmur rumbled through the crowd that had gathered. Near as I could tell, it was a murmur of approval, but I couldn't be sure. Maybe Pook had flaunted his cantankerous ways too long. Still, when the chips are down, a village—Indian or white—sticks by its own.

A third time Pook barked out his challenge.

"Why is Pook against me?" I said to Red Coal.

"White men killed Paiute two moons ago. Pook avenges the death," he replied.

I realized it would be a fight to the death. He intended to kill me. If I beat Pook, I was expected to kill him. If I failed to kill him,

I would be considered either a coward or it would be assumed that he had greater medicine than me.

Securing my rifle to the saddle, I swung my left leg over Mustang's withers and jumped to the ground. I don't know why, but Indians always dismount on the right side. They can't swing down because the stirrups, if they have any, aren't strong enough.

"Will the villagers stay off my back while I whip Pook?" I asked slowly. I had to talk slowly so that he could understand me. I thought I detected a slight grin on Red Coal's face, yet it seemed that he lacked confidence in my fighting skill.

"They have honor," he replied, "but give Red Coal message from his father before you fight. Red Coal think Pook kill Alma."

"That's a shame," I said, "because if he kills me, Posey's grandchildren won't get the message from their grandfather."

"Give Red Coal message," he insisted.

"*Kawtch* (no)!" I snapped. Turning, I walked directly toward Pook, drawing my Green River as I walked.

# CHAPTER 11
# RED COALS AND HOT POOK

My walk was straight and sure 'cause right then I was mad—mad at this hot-head named Pook who had caused me so much grief in the past months. Because of him, my coyote dun had given his life to save mine. I had fled across the natural bridge and been stranded for months.

For just a minute a flicker of doubt crossed my mind. One of man's greatest joys is to see growth in himself. I had grown much while stranded on the sacred mountain, had come to terms with myself and God. How could I possibly hate Pook for that? I shook the feeling off. Pook had challenged me to fight to the death and this was no time to doubt. In the next few minutes I must either kill Pook or be killed!

Pook was eyeing my Green River. I allowed myself a grin. It

wasn't a nice grin either 'cause I was feeling evil, ready to thrash the tar out of Pook by burying my Green River in his heart.

Maybe I was just full of pride, but there was nothing wrong with my fighting ability and I knew it. With Papa and Billy both as my trainers, I had no choice but to learn. When it came to fighting, Papa always said, "Just cuff your hat to a fightin' angle, boy, and crawl right in!"

His flint knife looked like a good one, but not nearly so long nor so sharp as my razor-sharp Green River. He was wearing only a loin cloth and moccasins and was approximately my height and weight. His brown skin glistened with a coat of fat and I wondered when he had taken time to smear himself. Maybe, I mused, he was one of the Indians I had seen wrestling from the ridge when I was studying the village. Indians often grease themselves when wrestling or fighting—makes them as slippery as greased pigs.

An angry breeze zipped through the camp like a whirlwind, stirring up the dust and removing a hat from one of the women. It reminded me of the breeze that suddenly came up on the mountain when Posey mentioned his father's name. For just a second I thought I heard Posey's soft chant.

In mid-stride I had an idea of how I could best win this challenge and gain the support of the village while doing so. Maybe it was placed there by the Great Spirit or the spirit of Posey. It was an idea that didn't include vengeance, but skill.

White men and Indians alike don't give the other culture the credit they deserve. Indians seem to hold white men in contempt and awe at the same time. They hold them in awe because of the wonders they possess, such as mirrors and fancy doodads. It must take powerful magic to make such wonders as mirrors. But at the same time they have contempt for white men because white men are so gullible as to give such magical items to a maiden for nothing more than a lover's stroll in the coolness of the afternoon.

White men hold Indians in contempt because they pray when they should fight, or think such items as a prayer stick or bear a claw necklace will make them invulnerable.

Likewise, in fighting styles, the two cultures generally don't give each other enough credit. 'Course, maybe I too wasn't giving credit where credit was due. Maybe I was underestimating my opponent, but I didn't think so. I had an idea he was pure poison in his own realm, but that he hadn't seen white men fight.

Returning my Green River to its sheaf, I returned to my mount and hung the weapon on the saddle. Then I stepped up to a warrior bystander and pointed to his knife. He guessed what I wanted and handed it to me. "*Ayyyh,*" someone uttered in approval. It was a word that I was not familiar with, but the rest of the crowd repeated it and I sensed a murmur of approval rippling through the crowd as I made my way to Pook. I had gained favor in the eyes of the villagers, but if I had miscalculated and should lose my life, it would amount to nothing.

We circled, as fighters do, and suddenly his foot came up and hit me a solid blow to the chest, a hallmark of Indian wrestling. Oh, he was quick! The blow would have knocked the wind out of me had I not seen it coming and set myself. I gave a quick slash with my knife, leaving his leg bloody, though just a flesh wound.

Again we circled and he jabbed right for my chest and belly. He was testing me, trying to read my style. I respected him for that, yet reading my style was something he should have done before he made the challenge.

The crowd was yelling something which I took to be words of encouragement to Pook. Surely they wouldn't be encouraging me more than one of their own. He dipped for a handful of dirt and in that instant I slid upwind. He almost missed me with the dirt, taking a little in his own face. I feigned and he jumped back, but recovered quickly, then drove his knife straight to my heart. I didn't step back but stepped in, slapping his arm aside and receiving a slash on my arm that cut clear through my buckskin sleeve.

Again we circled. I was bleeding a little and so was he. I wanted to grab for him the next time he thrust, yet I had fought greased Indians before and knew better than to even try. We both had weapons other than our knives: his weapon was his greased skin and mine was my thick buckskin clothing.

Most Indians are thrust-and-slash fighters when using flint knives. Even white men, with their steel knives, know better than to thrust in a knife all the way to the hilt, because it takes too much time to pull it out, time that could cost you your life. That is especially true with flint knives 'cause they are even harder to pull out.

Again Pook thrust and I slapped it aside. Seeing my chance at Pook's exposed side, I thrust in my knife, intending to pull my thrust and slice down after breaking the skin. But I miscalculated and the knife sunk in between Pook's ribs. With a quick twist, he turned, snapping off the point of my flint knife with his ribs.

Pook was wounded badly, though far from fatally. But I was in trouble—big trouble—because my knife no longer had a point. He cast me the nearest thing to a grin. He had me now, he thought.

The next time he thrust, I saw my opportunity. Keeping my body in line with him, I stepped back just long enough to take the force from his thrust, then stepped into him. His thrust was for my belly, just below my rib cage. But the front of my shirt was thicker than any Indian-made shirt and was padded with my linen shirt inside. I stepped into him, pinning his knife against my stomach. Luckily I had guessed correctly and the blade didn't penetrate. Maybe that surprised him, I don't know. It wouldn't have surprised him had he seen how my mother fashioned buckskin clothes.

Clasping the wrist of his knife hand with two hands, I put a big foot in his gut and rocked back to the ground, flipping him clear over my head. He recovered quickly, I'll have to grant him that, but he no longer had his knife. I did.

Leaning down, I slid the blade of the knife under my right foot and snapped it, then cast aside the pieces. Now the fight was in my territory. No weapons, just a toe to toe brawl!

He rushed, expecting to land a punch with his feet because Indians don't usually use their hands. Their hands are reserved for holding a weapon, so they use their feet. I slapped his foot aside and stepped in with a left jab that split his lips, showering him with blood. He looked furious, yet confused at the same time. I don't think he had ever seen boxing.

Pook recovered quicker than I had anticipated and landed a solid blow with his foot to my chest which sent me sprawling. He rushed, swinging a vicious kick, but I rolled out of the way and scrambled up, hurt and groggy.

Again he rushed, catching me with his slippery hand in a vicious head lock and twisted his hip into my body to pull me down. But the same grease that made his body so slippery made his arm too slick to hold me and I slipped out like a cork from a bottle. Spinning, I landed a left to his wind, a right to his heart, a second left to his wind, then I crumbled him up with a Liverpool kiss.

Stepping back to get my wind, I watched Pook stagger to his feet. But before he was set, I stepped in and boxed his ears with both hands. I saw a glassy look in his eyes. He looked like he was going to crumble.

I should have left him there, but I wasn't through. No siree! In my mind's eye I could see the eyes of my coyote dun horse, who gave her life that I might escape Pook and his kind. So I let loose with a right to the jaw that snapped his head back and rocked him to his toes. Then I followed through with a left to the wind and a solid right to the heart. He went down like a sack of potatoes.

The crowd was so silent you could hear a bee buzz. Maybe they had never seen that kind of fighting before. Fact is, I wasn't feeling so good myself 'cause Pook was no slouch when it came to fighting. I had to admire him for that.

Straightening to my full height, I looked around, the smell of battle in my nostrils. Red Coal stepped up to me and handed me my Green River. I knew I was expected to kill Pook; in fact, it was my duty. But I am beholden to only one man: God! So to heck with Indian tradition!

Looking into the crowd, my eyes rested on Red Coal. Looking

him squarely in the eye I said, "You need Pook when you fight the Navajos. I give him to you. I let him live."

"Pook has too powerful of medicine for you to kill him?" he asked.

I searched Red Coal's face, trying to detect if he was serious. He didn't sound like a Paiute. He sounded like an Arapaho or Apache, placing great stress on an individual warrior's medicine. Paiutes don't usually speak of individual warriors having powerful medicine, but then their shaman's teachings seemed to depart from the normal Paiute religion.

"Call it what you will," I replied, "but I've whipped him good. To kill him now when he is laying at my feet is not right by my standards."

Red Coal shrugged and the crowd murmured. I suspected I was making a fool of myself applying white man's values in a Paiute village.

Turning, I walked boldly to Pook's horse, standing quietly and wearing the saddle Pook had apparently taken from my coyote dun. It was my saddle and I aimed to have it back. Loosening the girth, I helped myself to the leather saddle. As the crowd mutely watched, I carried the saddle to Mustang and replaced Posey's Paiute saddle with my own.

As I watched, Red Coal commenced working over Pook. Apparently, Red Coal was somewhat of a community doctor. Several men and women combined their strength to carry Pook to a spot in front of Red Coal's wickiup. I suppose it took so many to carry him because his body was slippery with grease.

With practiced skill, Red Coal first set Pook's jaw. The warrior's ears were bleeding and he had a nasty gash on his lower jaw that was freely bleeding. Then as I watched, a squaw fetched some red coals on a rock. Skillfully using two stones to hold a hot coal, Red Coal touched the bleeder with a coal, chanting a smoothing chant as he worked. Not only did it stop the bleeding, but the pain brought Pook around.

All the time Red Coal worked, I was standing among the

crowd, a head taller than most of them. They didn't appear to either accept me or reject me; I was just there, a guest of Red Coal.

"Red Coal," I asked when we were at last able to resume our conversation, "is there anyone else in this village who hates white-eyes as did Pook?"

"Only his father, the shaman," he replied. "You should have killed Pook."

"Is that so important? I beat him."

"You fought well—showed great skill. But you have weak medicine and could not kill Pook. Warriors not afraid to fight Alma now. They will want to see if their medicine stronger than yours. I think they kill you."

Well, I had been told. It sounded like the old problem Shunktokecha had when one of the three Nephites told him not to count coup by killing. He was labeled a coward. Shunktokecha was my Father's Pawnee uncle. Oh well, I thought, I'm leaving Suhuh'vawdutseng Paiute country anyway.

"Give Red Coal message from my father," Red Coal pressed.

"My message is to show Posey's grandchildren some picture writings. How many children have you?"

"Red Coal has two sons. Why my father talk to you?"

"We were friends, thrown together by *Toovuts*, or maybe your grandfather's ghost," I replied, then spent the next half hour telling him what his father and I had done and seen together.

"Since Red Coal was a child, Father told him of the picture writings he saw as a child. No one else saw the writings, so villagers thought he was just talking."

"The writings are real."

"You stay here tonight. Tomorrow my sons and I go with you to see pictures."

"Will I be safe here?"

"You will be safe," Red Coal replied, but his words seemed to lack conviction. I had an idea that the usual honor of a Paiute village was hanging on the whims of a stone-hearted shaman.

"I think I will move on," I replied. "I want to start for my home, many suns away." I looked up at the sun, which had not yet reached the center of the sky. "Red Coal and sons come with Alma today!"

Red Coal looked me squarely in the eye as if he were looking into my very soul. Indians don't usually do that because many of them consider it rude. But I didn't avert my gaze, because if I did, he would have thought he had my soul. Medicine men can get away with many things that other Indians consider taboo.

After two or three minutes, Red Coal lowered his gaze and said, "I have only one horse."

"One son can ride behind you and one can ride with me," I offered.

Calling a son, Red Coal rattled off something in Paiute. The lad dashed off and returned a few minutes later with Red Coal's calico horse. Minutes later I swung into the leather, glad for the feel of my own saddle. Extending a hand to a big-eyed boy of six summers, I seated him behind me. The boy's name was Long Fingers, his baby name. Behind Red Coal was the lad that had fetched the horse. The older boy was tall and skinny and had soft, inquiring eyes. I later learned he had twelve summers, but had not yet been through his passage to manhood. His name was Cedar Eyes, which had something to do with his keenness of vision.

Walking our mounts through the village, I was surprised at how many women and children paused to watch us pass. There weren't many men in the village and I assumed that was because they were off trying to rustle up some game. There were several warriors clustered around a wickiup that I took for Pook's lodge. They cast me hard glances and I had an uneasy feeling.

We passed the shaman, standing with his hands on his hips. For just a moment I glanced into his eyes and didn't like what I saw: hatred. He seemed to be challenging me, mocking me.

We rode on but my thoughts were for the shaman and the evil I saw in his eyes. I wanted some way to tell him that his medicine wasn't so powerful. Maybe he practiced black magic and I suspect he did. But I was a child of God. Strange I should think of it that way—such a childish way for me to think, but so true.

But I didn't feel God-like, Christ-like, or even child-like. I felt like… "Oh, what the heck," I said aloud.

Red Coal cast me a curious glance. "What did you say?" he said.

"I said to wait here for a moment. I have unfinished business back in the village."

"With whom?" he said.

"Don't matter, just wait here."

"I go back with you."

"*Kawtch* (no)!" I spat out the words. "I don't want you to be connected with it!"

Lowering Long Fingers to the ground, I wheeled my mount around and returned to the village.

I have repeatedly been told by both Papa and Billy that you can always beat an Indian by using surprise. It's true with most whites, too, but particularly true with most Indians. And I had an idea.

As I neared the shaman war chief's lodge, he was fixing to mount his horse. The first thing that caught my attention was the bridle, 'cause it wasn't an Indian bridle, it was my bridle. And I had an idea he was fixing to follow me.

Bucking my mount to a stop, I cast him a winning smile and swung down. "Hold this, friend," I said, drawing my Green River and handing it to him hilt first.

Confused, the war chief took the knife, wonderingly. No sooner had he taken the knife, than I sent a solid left to his wind, followed by an uppercut to the jaw that lifted him to his toes and he dropped the knife. Then I followed through with a left, right, left, right, left and right to his mid-section, followed by a solid right to his heart that crumbled him to the ground.

"Just wanted you to know how I felt about things," I said, then reached for my Green River, replacing it in its scabbard. Stepping up to his horse I relieved it of my bridle, then swung into the leather of my mount and surveyed the surprised crowd. Allowing myself a grin, I wheeled my mount and cantered out of the village.

It was a dumb thing to do, I know, but I felt better.

As I reached the edge of the village, I saw Red Coal waiting for me. Apparently he had followed.

"I thought you were going to wait for me where I left you," I said.

"I thought you might need me and I'm glad I came," he replied. "I have never seen anyone with the nerve to tackle the shaman before."

Red Coal knew our general destination, so I allowed him to pick the route. As soon as we cleared the village, he made a sharp right turn and struck a game trail that seemed to lead over the mountain. Circling to the southwest, we traveled for several miles, then descended a steep juniper-covered slope.

After a while, Long Fingers started squirming and I suspected the saddle was pinching him. I pulled him in front and set him in the saddle with me. He sat there like he was used to sitting there and occasionally patted the old horse and jabbered to it. It occurred to me that he was used to riding on the old nag, probably in front of the grandfather.

When we crossed the wash, we followed it north and presently reached the familiar cliffs. I directed Red Coal to a rise on the left that offered a good view of Moroni's camp. I didn't have to point out the picture writings on the cliffs above, because Cedar Eyes had already discovered them and was pointing them out to his father.

"Why did Posey come to this lonely spot to live, away from his village and family?" I asked as Red Coal studied the writing.

"Him old man. Memory going. Came here to die."

I had guessed as much.

"Him talk much of picture writing when old," Red Coal continued. "He remembers boyhood things, but forgets his own name. Him say a white Indian that had lived since the old ones inhabited the land, pointed the writings out to him when he was a boy, before the trees grew in front of the writings. Villagers laugh at him."

"When my father was a boy," I replied, "he talked with a white Indian that was one of the old ones. We call him one of the Three Nephites."

Red Coal was starring at me. "Does such a one really live? How can it be?"

"Other tribes say that he lived," I replied. "Your father knew about him and called him Kokopelli—says he has lived for two thousand years. The picture writing on the cliff tells of him. When your people decide to make friends with the whites, there are many things we can learn from each other and other tribes, but nothing can be accomplished when you insist you have to kill each other to show honor."

"Your people kill our people for no reason. The shaman told us about that."

"And your people kill the whites for no reason, too. Did your shaman tell you that?"

"No, he didn't."

"Actually there is always a reason; it's just not a good reason that *Toovuts* or the white man's god would approve of. Enemy tribes have been killing each other long before white men arrived," I went on, fed up with my race being blamed for all of the Paiute problems. "Your father said you had a twin sister; what happened to her?"

"The Arapahos came down from the north and attacked our village. My sister and her warrior were newly married and were fleeing. Her warrior had on leggings with long fringes that became entangled in the brush and he couldn't go on. His wife stayed behind with him to help him get untangled, but by then the Arapahos were upon them and they killed both of them."

"Why were the Arapahos angry with your people? Why did they come down to kill?"

"There was no reason except that they despise my people because we have a strange religion. Besides, we were strangers and to be a stranger is the same as being an enemy."

"It sounds like things haven't changed much," I said.

Red Coal looked at me hard, knowing I was rebuking his people and maybe mine too, yet he had listened to my words. He said nothing, maybe thinking my words weren't worth a reply.

As if a great load had been lifted from my shoulders, I sensed that my mission was accomplished. I had honored Posey's dying request and could now turn Mustang's head west.

# CHAPTER 12
# A TINY SOUND

A belligerent wind whistled through the cottonwoods and to the west I heard the long howl of a wolf. Red Coal and his sons had chosen to spend the night at Posey's crude wickiup near the cliff. I had taken Mustang to the same little valley where Posey had kept her, then bedded down a hundred yards from Posey's brush lodge.

Something had awakened me and I lay listening. I wasn't alone. Straining all my senses, I became aware that the insects had quieted. Sliding my pistol into my hand, I waited.

There was a tiny sound of rock against rock, as if someone had stepped on a pebble. Glancing toward the source of the noise, a shadow moved, a tiny shadow. I put my pistol away as Long Fingers slipped under my rabbit-skin blanket beside me.

Had I not had an Indian brother and been somewhat trained

in Indian ways, I would not have understood. Long Fingers had been told that I was his grandfather's white brother and he had ridden with me on the horse that only his grandfather rode. The child accepted me as family.

When Indian children get cold at night, they share the body warmth of another family member, either child or adult. I had a blanket which he recognized as the one his grandfather used, but Red Coal and Cedar Eyes had nothing. So when the little tyke got cold, he knew where to go to get warm.

Not saying a word, Long Fingers burrowed deep under the rabbit-skin blanket, every inch of him. Then he lay still against my chest as he would have had I been Posey.

Listening intently to the sounds of the night, nothing seemed amiss. I pulled my blanket tighter around the two of us and returned to my slumber. I was fast asleep when She-Wolf's cold nose touched my face and I jumped, scared out of a week's worth of growth and she jumped too.

"She-Wolf," I muttered, tasseling her coat and drawing her to me, "if there's anything quieter than an Indian, it's you." She sniffed at Long Fingers, who reached out a tiny hand to stroke the pet. Then she lay down beside us, her head between her paws like a domestic dog. But wolves, like dogs, don't take long naps. So she was up and gone before morning.

Awakening with the birds, I shook out my boots to dislodge any creepy crawlies that might have settled in for the night. Then slid my feet into the boots and stomped them into place, leaving Long Fingers asleep in my blanket. Making my way to the pool below Snake Draw, I threw water on my face then observed my morning devotional.

As I was making my way back to the spot where I'd slept the night, Red Coal slid in beside me. He too had observed his morning devotional and was returning to Posey's lodge. In mid-stride he stopped, examining paw prints in the sand. I said nothing, waiting patiently, though I noticed that there were considerably more prints than one wolf could have made. It meant nothing to me, 'cept that She-Wolf's pack had held back while she came acalling.

Continuing to where I had left my gear and spent the night, Long Fingers looked out at us through sleepy eyes from under the blanket. Again Red Coal stopped and examined the wolf prints. 'Course, they were She-Wolf's prints.

Long and thoughtfully Red Coal read the signs. I patiently waited. Several times he glanced my way and once he carefully picked a wolf hair from my shirt, examining it.

"*Toovuts*," he muttered.

"*Peah' suhnuv* (big coyote)," I replied with a shrug. "See. There are the paw prints." *Toovuts*, a word reserved to God who was once a wolf, was misleading as the wolf was nothing more than a pet.

"Maybe you a trickster sent by *Soonungwuv*," he repeated. *Soonungwuv* is a god that was once a person but turned into a coyote and was something of a trickster.

"No, I am a man."

"Are you a Tookoov child?" The Tookoov people are the ones that built the cliff dwellings, but they are considered very short and sometimes Paiutes say they can hear them yelling in the mountains.

"No," I grinned, "I am too tall."

"Then you are a wolf man. A *kwetoo'unuv* (master wolf) by night and a man by day." I had heard of such a person.

"No!" I replied. "I am a man all the time!"

"Then why do you leave wolf prints and why does the wolf tribe come to visit you?" he asked, taking a backwards step away from me. "I think you either trickster or wolf-man who turns into a wolf when the sun dips below Earth Mother. You are the wolf-man my father spoke of."

Allowing myself a grin, I set him straight with the simple explanation, "I have a wolf friend named She-Wolf, nothing else." Then I told him how She-Wolf and I were thrown together by circumstances. He listened attentively as I spoke. My usage of the Paiute language was clearly more graceful than when I first met

Posey.

"You were the Toohoov child that gave my father the strange animal?" he asked, referring to the pig I had lowered to Posey.

"Uh-huh," I replied, giving up on the conversation. He looked at me, wondering what that meant, because in Paiute, *uh-huh* means yes, not no. "I gave Posey the pigmy pig but I am not a Toohoov child," I repeated and he nodded.

"Maybe," he muttered, "villagers not find it so easy to kill you."

"Villagers will never see me again," I replied. "I only went there to honor your father's dying wish. I will never see them again."

"Don't be so sure," he replied.

# CHAPTER 13
# WE GO HUNTING

With most Native Americans, time means almost nothing, and apparently the Paiutes were no different. It's a somewhat whimsical life. If you're happy, you keep doing what you're doing. If not, you do something else.

It was Cedar Eyes who made the suggestion. Eyeing my rifle, he asked, "We go hunting?" Both he and Red Coal were looking at me and I knew what they were getting at. There likely weren't many rifles available at the village and standing a hundred yards away, shooting at a deer is much easier than creeping within bowshot range from the downwind side of a wily buck. I nodded my consent and saw Red Coal smile for the first time. The hunt was planned for the next morning.

We woke with the birds, which is generally about an hour

before sunlight. Then we moved out in the predawn darkness, all four of us. Dawn still hadn't come when Red Coal positioned me on a low ledge that overlooked a saddle, heavy with sagebrush and deer browse and dotted with bright red Indian paint brush. He and Cedar Eyes slipped into the darkness to stir up whatever animals might be there. My task was to harvest any game that crossed the saddle.

With me was Long Fingers, his legs being too small to keep up with his father and brother. I'll have to hand it to the little tyke, when his father told him to be quiet, he didn't make a peep. It's the only thing Paiute children are strictly disciplined in.

The spot Red Coal had chosen for the hunt was north of the cliffs. In the starlight I could see the sacred mountain and the corn field where the pygmy boars lived, several miles to the south.

The birds were incredibly noisy as they ushered in the new day. The Great Silence is only truly silent on the Great Plains where there are few or no birds. The animals of the night were seeking their holes. A wolf spider zipped under a rock and a wasp winged past. The whole hillside was making the change from night to day.

Below the ridge to my right was a field of moon-lilies. As the morning dawned, the white trumpet flowers began to close. As I watched them close, I caught movement and raised my rifle, but it was only a coyote climbing to the saddle from my right. When he hopped out of the saddle, he sniffed the breeze, then wheeled and returned the way he had come.

Straining to see what had startled him, I saw four deer coming over the saddle. The coyote surely wouldn't be shy of deer, so he must have caught the scent of Red Coal or Cedar Eyes. The deer weren't running all out, though they were moving at a lively walk. They represented enough meat to last Red Coal's family for a long time, providing he jerked it and didn't give it to the rest of the village to eat up fast in an impromptu feast. But that was none of my concern.

I seem to do best when firing at a string of game if I move from left to right rather than right to left, so I rested my sights on the far left deer and waited. When all were lined up the way I wanted them, I squeezed off the first round and felt the weapon leap in my hands. Quickly I levered a second, then third round and let the rifle do the job for which it was made.

All four deer took off running, but one by one the first three stumbled and went down, 'cause there was nothing wrong with my aim. I hadn't had a clear shot at the fourth deer, which made it into the junipers.

Long Fingers was excited. Oh, was he excited! He could hardly keep from squealing with delight. He started jumping up and down like a barrel boundin' down the hill, yet he kept his mouth tightly closed.

"You don't have to be quiet anymore," I said, grinning. "If there are any other deer around, they're running away from the sound."

He followed me as we approached the game, then he squealed with delight, as a white boy might. One by one I cut each deer's throats and was surprised to see that the third deer was a nursing doe. Generally, fawns stop nursing in the summer. Yet, like human babies, there are some fawns that feel the need to suck as long as the mother deer will let them suck. But somewhere was a fawn, waiting for his mother to return, though he surely was old enough to survive without mother's milk.

Red Coal and his son found us and we began the butchering. When Indians or most mountain men butcher, the first thing they do is remove the liver and eat it raw as they work. You can imagine how bloody Long Fingers' face was as he was eating his share of the liver, because little people, regardless of race, seem to be adept to getting into their food. I struck a fire and cooked one of the livers for me 'cause I like the sweetness of cooked meat, though I still wanted it red inside.

When the meat was ready to be transported, I told Red Coal to use both mounts to transport the meat while Long Fingers and I back tracked the nursing doe afoot, trying to find her fawn. They agreed and I fully expected them to take the meat all the way back to their village so that the women could cure it. To my surprise, I learned a few hours later that they took the meat to the cottonwoods by the cliffs, but not too close to Posey's lodge. There they jerked a large quantity while Long Fingers and I hunted for the fawn.

For having only six summers, Long Fingers was good at backtracking the doe. Her hooves were a little smaller and more pointed than the other two deer and generally she had been in the rear. We crossed a pool of stagnant water and washed the blood from Long Fingers' face.

It took us nearly three hours and it was Long Fingers who eventually found the fawn by imitating a mother deer, something I had never heard before. Fawns are always tender and make good eating, but if Indian children can get lone fawns to eat tender twigs and grasses, they make pets out of them. Naturally that is what Long Fingers wanted to do. She was a big fawn, but you can't tie a leash around a fawn's neck and expect her to follow you unless she has been trained. So I draped the critter over my shoulders and we started for Posey's wickiup.

For the third night in a row, Long Fingers slept with me and I admit that I was beginning to feel a little protective of him. Nothing in my life had prepared me for that type of an experience. She-Wolf spent much of the night with us. Maybe she was feeling protective, too.

On the morning of the fifth day, I awoke wondering what had awakened me. A low snarl came from She-Wolf and suddenly I realized the Great Silence was almost upon us. Glancing in the direction the wolf was looking, I saw Red Coal.

"Quiet," Long Fingers said, patting the wolf. She-Wolf accepted her reprove, but didn't like Red Coal.

"You better back up," I said to Red Coal. "The wolf doesn't know you." Red Coal backed up and She-Wolf seemed to feel better.

"She-Wolf likes you," I said to Long Fingers, amazed at the calming influence he had on the wolf.

"Me got two pets," he said, "wolf and fawn."

"Wolves and fawns don't get along," I replied.

"We teach them to be friends," he stated.

"Good idea, but how are you going to do that?" If anyone could do it, it seemed that Long Fingers could.

"You hold wolf. I get fawn," he said as he scampered off. When next he appeared, he had the fawn on a leash. But suddenly the fawn caught the wolf's scent and pulled away, despite all the six-year-old could do. Running to Long Finger's rescue, Cedar Eyes caught the fawn and tied her to a scrawny juniper.

Scrambling to where I waited, Long Fingers said, "Take wolf to fawn."

Well, I didn't know about that, but it wasn't my show. I wasn't sure She-Wolf would stay with us. She might bound across the wash. Still, Long Fingers and I started for the fawn, She-Wolf between us.

We moved twenty paces, but the fawn was straining so hard against the leash we thought she might choke herself. So we stopped for a time and the little critter calmed.

"This may take time," I said. "Maybe your fawn will break the leash."

"Why she so scared? Wolf our friend."

"I don't know why. Maybe the fear of wolves is inbred?"

Long Fingers looked at me, not understanding my words. I wasn't sure I understood.

Slowly we closed the gap, twenty paces at a time. Each time we moved, the fawn went wild, trying to pull away. Then we'd hold our position while Long Finger ran to the fawn and calmed her.

We had closed more than half the distance to the fawn and seemed to be making real progress. Then suddenly the fawn stopped balking and dropped in her tracks.

"Go to her," I whispered. "Maybe she choked herself and needs the leash loosened." Long Fingers scampered off. Reaching the fawn, he pulled on her, telling her to get up. Then he dropped to his knees and hugged her.

As She-Wolf and I waited, there was growing realization that the pet wasn't going to get up...at least not soon. Still, we waited.

She-Wolf was uneasy, ready to return to the hills for another day. So I bade her goodbye and she bounded off across the wash to the juniper-covered hills.

Long Fingers was hugging the fawn when Red Coal and I approached. The lad's eyes were moist and he was having a hard time keeping his face straight, 'cause Paiute boys are taught not to cry.

The fawn was dead.

"Why my fawn die?" he asked. "Why? Why?"

"Maybe fright," Red Coal replied.

"Wolf didn't hurt her!" the lad insisted. "Wolf wasn't even close."

Red Coal knelt down beside his son and I left them to have a father-son chat. As I walked away, I wasn't as good as Long Fingers at keeping the tears from my eyes. I was like that fawn. Every time I rode into an Indian village, I established a preconceived notion of how I would be treated and I wasn't usually wrong.

# CHAPTER 14
# SUDDENLY MY REVOLVER BUCKED

Lively, I stepped out with a purpose, making my way to the tiny valley where Mustang waited. Passing by the pool beneath Snake Draw, I gave the cliffs a final scrutiny, casting for the hand and foot holes and remembering my harrowing descent. The dry waterfall rose, majestic and brooding, topped with a dry spillway and an ancient gnarled juniper that I had looped my rope around on my first descent.

Crossing the wash I followed the bank, zigzagging between the junipers. Making a right turn up a slope and suddenly I knew something was wrong. It was far too quiet. The very silence was menacing, the stillness a warning.

I fell to the ground and just lay there, listening. Nothing.

Moving with the waves of grass, I made my way up the slope

to the saddle and eased to a juniper tree where I could get a view. Sliding under the tree I parted the grass for a look at the open slope below and was brought up short.

Three Paiute warriors!

Farther back, framed against some junipers, were a dozen more Paiutes. All seemed to be warriors. Apparently they had been waiting for me, easily guessing my route because there weren't very many ways to get from Posey's lodge to the little valley where I kept Mustang. They were just sitting on their horses, their faces showing no expression. Nothing about them suggested friendship.

Glancing down the slope the way I had come, I didn't see anything. A bird lit in the brush maybe a hundred feet below me and started preening his feathers. Then suddenly he took off, straight up, or so it seemed. Clearly there were Indians down there.

Returning my gaze to the three warriors in front of me, I moved out from under the juniper and stood up. Slowly I lowered my trappings to the ground and in the same smooth move flipped the thong from my revolver and loosened it in its holster. I knew what they wanted.

A horse stomped and another blew, but no one moved for a full minute. Then one warrior swung his leg over his mount and jumped to the ground, followed by the other two warriors. The Paiutes farther back, silhouetted against the trees, started circling me.

I was trapped and I knew it. Yet when I went down, I intended to take a parcel of Paiutes with me.

This was to be a contest, of that I was certain. It was a contest on their part to see who had the skill to kill me, a warped sense of bravery. In a way they were showing me honor, but when it was over I would be just as dead.

The center warrior drew his knife and the other two each held a bow with a quiver of arrows on their backs. The bow was one of those bows made from juniper wood and the arrow was one of those current wood arrows with a fire hardened wooden point tied onto its split end with sinew and I suspected the point was poisoned. Paiutes sometimes make arrows poison by boiling rabbit blood with salt. Other times they make it out of the blue in a rabbit's liver. Either way you are just as dead, but it is a slow death. I suspected the center warrior would fight me first; the other two were just to insure a contest took place. Had any of them seen how fast a man can draw a revolver? I thought not. I recalled that Posey had never seen one before.

The other two warriors fit arrows to bow strings. The arrows were, of course, to shoot into my arms and legs if I decided not to fight, as they didn't want me to die quickly.

This was stupid, really stupid! I was getting mad—mad and irritated. What made them think they had a right to force me to play their life and death games? 'Course, maybe I was selling them a little short.

Casting a pleading prayer toward heaven, I forced myself to relax, at the same time steeling my nerves against all outside interference. If I died, I died. There are worse things than a quick death in battle.

The air smelled of dust, probably from the movement of the Paiute horses. Touching my tongue to my lips, I realized that my mouth was dry. I needed to relax more, so I took just a minute to become at one with nature, noticing the fuzzy yellow flowers on the catclaw that grew behind the Paiutes and a stately yucca with several yucca moths hovering around. I allowed the tension to drain from my muscles and took several deep breaths. Pulling myself to my full height, I worked my fingers and zeroed my concentration in on my opponents. I was ready.

The center warrior dropped to a crouch and motioned for me to come to him. I shook my head in disgust and waited, straight and tall, but with my empty right hand near my revolver, ready for a draw should anyone try to release an arrow.

Exasperated, the warrior made a slight thrusting motion, but still I stood my ground. He was starting to get enraged and I smiled at that, 'cause when you're too enraged, you don't think straight.

"Squaw!" he snapped.

I smiled and that angered him more.

"Coward!" he screamed, growing bold with rage. At least I thought the word he said was coward, but it didn't much matter what it was.

The warrior on the left drew his bow string tight. This is it, I thought. This is the time to act!

Suddenly my revolver bucked in my hand and I barely remembered drawing.

The principle of fast drawing is the same as the principle of Indian offhand shooting. It usually takes two shots—the first to see where your bullet goes and the second to zero in. But there is seldom an error with your vertical plane; the error comes only in your horizontal plane. A gunfighter may dust his opponent's feet or even shoot the hat from the head on his first shot, but his vertical plane—as well as his second shot—will be right on and deadly.

Well, I took the warrior on the left in the chest, though my eyes were focused on the sour grin across his face. His arrow zinged off to who-knows-where.

The right-hand warrior took my bullet in the right side of his chest 'cause I had to swing my weapon to the right and was off a little vertically. The warrior with the knife took my slug squarely in the teeth. I had fired so close together that the reports of all three shots seemed to bounce off the hills in one long, easy roll.

But I didn't stop there, 'cause once you get your mind into the fighting mode, you don't always know when to stop. I swung and took out a mounted warrior behind me, an ominous looking fellow whose commanding presence showed through as he set his mount. And I would have kept killing until I was killed had I not heard Red Coal's high-pitched scream yelling for me to stop.

I stopped, but I held my pistol in readiness, at the same time extracting four shells from my cartridge belt and feeding them into the cylinder.

Red Coal slid in beside me, reprimanding his fellow tribesmen and talking far too rapidly for me to catch every word. Yet I knew some of what he said. He said they had attacked his guest and had violated Paiute laws regarding guests. They had displeased *Toovuts*.

The next thing he told them I could hardly understand at all. I picked up the word *Toovuts* again and the word *Kwetoo'unuv* (master wolf) but didn't know what he said about the wolf because, as I said, he was speaking far too rapidly for me.

The tension seemed to be easing, but I knew the women would be wailing the death chant in their lodges 'cause I had taken out four warriors. Nothing in my mind was more morbid than the death chant, yet what else could I have done?

Sliding my loaded .44 into its holster, but not feeling secure enough to attach the thong, I made my way to the dead warrior's mounts. The mounts were mine to my way of thinking and by Indian customs they were the spoils of battle. Yet I remembered the skimpy herd of mustangs near the village and decided I didn't need the mangy animals as much as they did. Behind one of the saddles was my woolen blanket, rolled inside my slicker. I claimed my property.

In the distance a wolf howled and I listened for answering calls. The Paiutes were also listening, studying me intently. Red Coal was especially studying me.

Glancing at my pistol, he said, "Little gun jumped into master's hand." But instead of "little gun," the words he used could be better translated as "baby gun."

"That's what your father said when he saw me draw," I replied. "He had never seen a little gun before."

"Neither have I, but our shaman has. He spoke of seeing them during the Black Hawk War."

Warriors had begun tying the bodies of the dead on their horses, occasionally casting me sidelong glances as they worked. I didn't altogether trust them and wondered what they were thinking.

"Will others from your village come to fight me?" I asked Red Coal. I had noticed that he had not left my side, almost as if he were acting as my bodyguard.

"No," he replied. "The man whom you shot on the horse when you whirled around after shooting your three opponents was the war chief."

"You mean the shaman? I know the shaman and it wasn't him!"

"Yes, it was him. He was just painted up so much that you didn't recognize him. And the warrior holding the knife was Pook's brother. The other two were henchmen."

"What does that mean?" I asked, trying to grasp the whole situation as I spoke.

"That means you have wiped out the leaders of the rowdies in our village," he replied, "and convinced the village that Pook and his friends were not the warriors that they claimed to be."

"It's a good thing to rid a village of rowdies," I replied, "but next time you fight the Navajos or the Arapahos, or whomever you fight, you will miss them."

"Maybe," he replied, "we need to be a more peaceable village, not so quick to judge strangers and kill them."

I nodded. He was beginning to sound down-right non-Indian. I was beginning to see the light. Now if only white men could learn those truths.

# CHAPTER 15
# THE LOBO LOPED OVER THE RISE

Hoping that Red Coal could keep his villagers off my back in case they had a change of heart, I turned my back on them and made my way up a ridge. I figured on circling to the tiny walled valley where Mustang was kept. At the top of the rise I picked up my trappings and threw them across my right shoulder. In my left hand was my Winchester, but I kept my right hand free and close to my revolver. Turning to the west, I circled to another ridge, one that I had never been over before, but I was just passing through.

As I topped the ridge, straight ahead, not a hundred feet away, a lone wolf was making its way up from the other side, headed directly toward me. We were a hundred feet apart when we saw each other and at about the same instant we both froze in our tracks. Twice the size of She-Wolf, it was a large timber wolf that easily weighed a hundred-fifty pounds. The folks in Manti called such a wolf a "lobo." As I considered, I realized this was the area I had seen a wolf from up on the cliff, many weeks earlier.

The lobo wolf wasn't scared of me, not so's you'd notice, nor was I scared of it. But there is no sense asking for trouble. Where you see one wolf, another one is not far away.

Glancing back over my shoulder, the Paiutes were watching me and I dismissed the idea of returning the way I had come. To the left seemed my best route, so dropping over the crest of the ridge, I turned to the left, making my way to Mustang's valley corral. Weary, the lobo watched me. Only when I had proceeded some distance just below the crest of the ridge did the wolf continue.

Wolves seldom attack people unless it's the dead of winter and they are hungry, but still I was wary, repeatedly casting backward glances to the meat eater. I proceeded on up the next ridge and as I was about to top out, it occurred to me that the wolf and the Indians were both in for a big surprise, so I turned for a look.

I watched the lobo lope up the rise, then skid to a stop atop the ridge. Having seen the Paiutes, he cast a glance my direction and I grinned, knowing what he was thinking. For several moments he studied the Indians, occasionally glancing in my direction, then made up his mind to mosey the other direction, ready to bound away at the slightest threat.

I wondered what the Indians were thinking, allowing a grin to cross my lips. It seemed good to feel the tension drain from me and I allowed myself an all-out chuckle. Continuing to Mustang's valley, there was an added spring to my step.

Mustang nickered as I approached and jumped down the sandstone outcropping. It wasn't impossible for her to break out of the walled valley, though it was ringed with ledges, but she lacked reason. A tiny spring crossed a meadow of sweet grass, spilling into the wash at the far end of the valley, where Posey had drug deadfalls to create a corral. Outside was nothing but coarse burro grass and woolfat for the horse to eat.

Why Posey had not camped there, I don't rightly know, but supposed that he had gone off away from his horse to die. Some Paiutes want to take the spirit of their favorite pony with them when they die, but apparently Posey didn't feel that way. Maybe he attached sacred significant to his camping spot at the base of the sacred mountain. Or maybe he didn't want the meat-eaters to be attracted to his body after he died, or to take a notion to munch down on his horse. Wolves don't generally attack mustangs, as mustangs are from wild stock and can generally hold their own, unless there is a whole pack of wolves.

"How ya doing, old girl," I muttered as I fussed over Mustang. She bobbed her head playfully in a romping mood. I fussed over her like a child and she liked it.

Saddling up, I swung into the leather from the left side, like a white man. Mustang was weary and balked halfheartedly, as it was a strange way for her to be mounted. We had a long way to go together and I wasn't going to mount her Indian style forever.

Patting her withers to settle her, I turned her head toward the wash. I had it in mind to catch one last glimpse of Moroni's camp before I turned west and bid goodbye to Red Coal, Cedar Eyes, and especially Long Fingers, if'n I could find them.

Walking Mustang up the wash, she shied at a skinny brown rattler, the type seen up on the mountain. Different from most of the rattlers I'd seen on the valley floor, I presumed it had been washed down Snake Draw and over the watercourse by a flash flood. Bypassing the rattler, I walked Mustang on up the wash to the pool at the base of Snake Draw, allowing her to drink before our long, dry journey west.

With no signs of Red Coal, Long Fingers, Cedar Eyes or their mount, I turned Mustang's head toward a view spot a quarter mile west and once there I swung down, allowing myself one last, lingering view of the pictographs at Moroni's camp. Mustang was looking to the right, so I suspected someone, probably Red Coal or one of his sons, had found me and was making his way up through the junipers. Still I checked the load in my revolver and returned it to its holster.

Red Coal and his sons timidly approached, almost apologetic, as if not knowing if they should bother me as I studied Moroni's Camp.

"Two men on cliff," Red Coal spoke in Paiute. I had been watching the cliff and hadn't seen anyone. If there were men on the cliff they would have to be ghosts, so I glanced curiously at Red Coal. I didn't discount his words, 'cause generally speaking, Indians are more spiritually intense than white men. When they fast and pray, which they do often, though always alone, they often claim to see visions, usually in the smoke of the fires. Indians who 1are cruel are very cruel and those who are spiritual are very gentle and spiritual. White men know that they never see visions and they are not disappointed. But Indians actually believe they will see visions and claim that they do.

"You turned back into man," he continued. It was a statement, not a question.

"What?" I questioned.

"You had turned into a wolf, but now you have turned back into a man."

"Red Coal!" I snapped. "I was never a wolf!"

"Warriors saw you turn into wolf," he defended. "I saw you. My sons saw you."

I glanced at Cedar Eyes, then at Long Fingers. Both boys were innocent and trusting, ready to accept me regardless of my human or animal state. Here was a family to stand beside a man, a family that had inched their way into my heart. And I had only known them a week.

"None of you saw me turn into a wolf," I explained. I spoke slowly and clearly so that none would misunderstand. "You saw me disappear over the ridge a short while before a timber wolf appeared."

Red Coal's steady gaze looked into my soul, like he had tried to do once before. This time it was I that turned away and I glanced to the pictographs, then looked again.

Two men were at Moroni's camp, just standing there, looking our direction. One looked surprisingly like Posey and the other was wearing something that looked suspiciously like a breast plate.

Blinking, I looked again, but they were gone. Glancing at Red Coal I saw the nearest thing to a mischievous smile I had ever seen on any Indian, 'cept for Billy and he doesn't count.

I shook my head to clear it. I was beginning to think like Posey and Red Coal. It was high time for me to swing into the leather and skedaddle for home.